DUTY TO WARN

DUTY TO WARN

A NOVEL

SARA KERSTING

ACRE

CINCINNATI 2018

Acre Books is made possible by the support of the Robert and Adele Schiff Foundation.

Library of Congress Cataloging-in-Publication Data have been applied for.
ISBN-10 (pbk): 1-946724-10-6 / ISBN-13 (pbk): 978-1-946724-10-6
ISBN-10 (ebook): 1-946724-11-4 / ISBN-13 (ebook): 978-1-946724-11-3

Designed by Barbara Neely Bourgoyne
Cover art: Nicholas A. Tonelli, *Country Road*, 2012

This is work of fiction. Names, characters, businesses, places, events, locales, and incidents are either products of the author's imagination or used in a fictitious manner. Any resemblance to actual persons, living or dead, or actual events is purely coincidental.

The press is based at the University of Cincinnati, Department of English and Comparative Literature, McMicken Hall, Room 248, PO Box 210069, Cincinnati, OH, 45221–0069. www.acre-books.com

Acre Books books may be purchased at a discount for educational use. For information please email business@acre-books.com.

To my husband, Jim, who gave me the space
and time to write by bicycling across the country
four times in the years it took me to finish.

DUTY TO WARN

1

MALDEN

It wasn't the first time David Malden felt paralyzed by a patient, but the last time was so long ago he couldn't remember it. Thirty years of providing psychological services had taught him when to speak, when to be still, how to redirect the flow of communication. Malden was good at the job; he was patient; he knew how to wait for words that would come, emerging sometimes in spite of the speaker—words to repeat, consider, use. Initially just one or two, but if things went right, there would be more and more of these words, and then the work could begin.

Often progress happened slowly, but with Robert Percy, it wasn't happening at all. For a month and a half, the man never missed a session, sat hunched in the chair as if the faded sweatshirt and denim jacket weighed him down, his large sad eyes fixed on Malden's face. The weeks passed, the old snow in the streets of Buffalo melted in the cold rain of upstate New York spring, and Robert Percy never stopped talking. His story was always the same: he had no friends and no family, except for a foster mother in Michigan. Everyone—where he worked, where he lived, where he ate, where he shopped—treated him unfairly, or worse, ignored him. He tried to make friends, and Malden could imagine how: following people around, sticking to them until they had to shake him loose, doing favors, lending things, buying things so he had them to lend. Like a kid offering you his toys if you'll just let him play.

But Robert Percy wasn't a kid. He was almost thirty, according to the notes Sonja gave Malden. He was taller than Malden and much heavier, twice as wide in the shoulders, burly in a soft, helpless way.

Nothing Malden said or suggested had worked, but he had no illusions about why. Robert Percy couldn't afford to change. If people treated him differently, it would upset the balance. And so far, Malden had no idea why the balance was so crucial. Percy was proving to be more competent at maintaining his helplessness than Malden was at uncovering its source.

He stared at Robert Percy. The man never stopped to breathe.

"Most likely a simple case of depression and anxiety," Sonja had told him, her small eyes watching him, like she watched everything, carefully. "Not serious enough for us over at the hospital." She glanced around his office. "I thought you could use a change from the affluent divorcées." The comment stung, as she knew it would.

Percy was more than a change. When he first showed up, Malden thought he'd come to fix something. Sonja said he worked at Bosworth's, one of the manufacturing plants south of the city where she occasionally gave presentations for the employee assistance program. Robert Percy approached her after she'd finished a session on anger management. Malden wondered what those men thought of Sonja Nielsen, a tall, large-boned woman with a small pale oval of a face, a flat voice sure of its own way. It was her body they would remember, big and strong-looking, shoulders that would bear, carry, endure. In a long dress and a bonnet, Sonja Nielsen would have walked alongside oxen. As it was, she favored cheap pantsuits, regardless of weather or fashion—like some kind of security guard, he'd told her once, but she just shrugged.

It was time to call her, set up a consultation. Malden had put it off long enough.

Percy was in the middle of a story about a girl at the plant, the one who worked in the office and had seemed so nice, before. But she made a face when Percy asked for a change in his schedule. "She asked me if I thought I was special. She made her voice funny when she said *special*." Percy kept his eyes on Malden's face. "The other woman laughed."

Malden cleared his throat. "Do you . . ."

"I don't think she was teasing. Maybe, but I don't think so." Percy bowed his head, probably the same way he had then, and Malden was left staring at the man's shaggy reddish hair. A moment later, when Percy lifted his head and started to talk, Malden said, "Wait."

Percy waited, and Malden waited too. He wasn't sure why. When Percy opened his mouth again, Malden just shook his head. Percy swallowed, blinked, and looked down at his hands. When he glanced up and started to say something, Malden shook his head again. Malden had no plan. He had nothing to say, but he couldn't let Percy talk. He was done with words.

Percy studied his shoes, shifted in his chair. He peered at Malden's face, looked away, confused. Malden held himself very still. He heard a car door slam in the parking lot; he heard a phone next door; he heard Percy breathing, heavily now.

Then Malden heard a different sound, not really a sound, more like a very low tone, a hum, but then it grew in volume, and Malden realized it was coming from Percy. His eyes were shut and his mouth was closed, his lips pressed tightly together, but the sound got louder.

Malden seldom touched a patient, but he reached over now, placing his hand on the man's shoulder. Percy opened his eyes, and then he opened his mouth, but the sound that came out took Malden by surprise. He expected a roar, a scream, a cry. It was all of that, but none of that, because there was no sound. It was a huge scream that made no sound at all.

NIELSEN

I hadn't known what I was waiting for, until it didn't happen. It was June before I heard anything from Malden about Robert Percy, and that was only because I spotted Malden during a coffee break at a local conference, this one on bipolar issues. I didn't have to corner him; he had already done that himself, moved one of the chairs to the back of the room, as far as possible from the tables of coffee and tea and the people who surrounded them.

Malden would have seen me long before, towering over the other women. I was used to the looks I got. Neither rail-thin nor heavy, I inspired not envy, not pity, but a cross between curiosity and wariness, as if my size implied some slight danger.

Malden always appeared out of place in a crowd of psychologists, counselors, and social workers—not at all like a man to whom you would bare your soul, entrust your guilt, your shame, your stupidities. He didn't have the face for it. His skin was too pale, his eyes too dark, and they seemed to glitter strangely at times, making you wonder what he was seeing. His mouth was wide but his lips thin, and he had a way of pressing them together that marked him as a man not easily pleased.

But he was successful with patients, in spite of his demeanor and the current preference for warm and tender therapists. Malden was intelligent, perceptive, willing to consider unorthodox or unpopular theories, but none of that seemed as essential as the way he would focus on a patient and a problem. As if nothing else were more important, as if nothing occupied him beyond what you were saying, what you thought, what you had done, what you were considering doing. Who wouldn't improve, experiencing that degree of attention?

When I asked about Robert Percy, he frowned. "It's not a simple case." He looked at me as if I had known that, eyeing me so closely that for a moment I wondered if maybe I had.

"I missed that," I admitted.

He nodded. "It took some time."

That's when the bell rang to resume the session, so I had only a few minutes to hear about Percy, against the background of conference room noises. That's what I remember—not Malden's voice, which tends to go flat, nearly toneless, when he describes a case, as if he is trying to distance himself from symptoms, from suffering—but the soft clink and rattle of cups and spoons, the murmuring of a well-dressed crowd, refreshing themselves.

What I learned was more than enough to occupy my thoughts for the next hour, to the exclusion of the speaker I had come to hear. At one point I turned and glanced behind me, but Malden's chair was empty.

I was sure of a call to consult after that, but not because I had doubts about Malden's skills or experience. He had worked with child abuse cases before. It's a lonely and delicate job, a balancing act between the past and the present. Sometimes you can get trapped back there, feeling so battered and wounded yourself from the stories, the cruelties, that you lose direction. These weren't recovered memories, Malden said; they were right there, and he knew he wasn't the first person, or maybe even the tenth person, to hear them. Though he suspected he was the first person to hear them all.

"Percy must feel a strong connection to you," I said. Malden looked away and shrugged, but I knew what that meant, and maybe he was right, maybe it was just the right time and Malden's office, for all that I've scorned it, was the right place.

It was months later, early August, the air in Buffalo thick with humidity, before I heard from him. His office was not that far a drive, but felt a world away from mine at the hospital. Discreetly nestled in a quiet suburb, the group practice occupied one of a small collection of medical buildings disguised by weathered brick, colonial shutters, and expensive landscaping. Malden's office was on the first floor, the rest of MacAllister's group on the second.

His decor wouldn't be my choice—the carpet pale, the paint quiet, the artwork soothing. "Neutered," I joked once, and Malden looked at me sharply. The only sign of real life was a kid's drawing, trees like lollipops, flowers the same size as the stick people. That and the photo on the desk of Amy, grown now, graduating from high school, Joan standing next to her—a mother-daughter portrait.

I knew Amy was in Spain, a college junior on a year abroad; I wanted to ask how she was doing, but Malden was already looking at his watch, his face more colorless than usual. He could look unnerving at times. I dropped into the soft upholstery of a large armchair, thought about the aged plastic seats in my office, and wondered if

Malden ever missed those years at the hospital. We had been a good team.

He stood in front of his desk, studying a stack of files. "I need for you to take over two cases for me, just for a few weeks, maybe less. I'll speak to MacAllister about it."

"Amy?" I asked. It wouldn't be unusual, a relapse, Madrid too far from home, too soon, or maybe just the added stress of travel. Perhaps there had been a change in medications.

"No, this isn't about her." He picked up two of the files. "She's coming home, sometime this month, soon."

"Earlier than planned, then?" I wasn't just being curious; I had an investment in this young woman, but one I couldn't discuss with Malden.

"I don't have much time. I'm leaving tonight." Malden moved into the opposite armchair, set the files down on the small table between us.

"I'm not helping unless I know why, Malden."

He leaned forward, put his hands up to his face, rubbed his eyes for a long moment. In the old days I would have reached over and grabbed his arm, told him to give it a rest.

"I'm driving to Michigan," he said finally. "Robert Percy left a message on Saturday, saying he had to leave town. I didn't get it till Monday. I called his workplace. Percy told them on Friday he had to go home, to Michigan. Said there had been a death in the family. I called the number he listed for next of kin, a foster mother, Helen Johnson. She's alive and well."

Malden stared at me, his eyes dark holes. "There is no 'family,' Sonja. There were ten families, maybe more, and significant abuse in at least five. I have names." He gestured back at his desk. "Names of people, names of towns."

I didn't say anything. It must have been the look on my face that sent him back over to his desk. He came back with a small tape recorder, set it on the table, and pressed a button. "Listen," he said. "Just listen."

I didn't recognize Percy. His voice was distorted by rage, at times low, guttural, as if lodged deep within his body. Other times, it was pitched high, shrill, like the tones of a small child. And in the background, always, the sounds of pounding, stomping, Percy's fists against the chair, Percy's boots on the floor, obliterating something only he could see.

Malden stopped the tape. "It was like this for months, then something changed. He started to miss appointments. He quit talking . . . about them." Malden rubbed his forehead. "Percy called me Thursday night, late, but my cell phone was off. I didn't check till Friday, late Friday. He said he just wanted to talk. I tried calling back, but no one answered. Percy doesn't have a cell phone. He must have called from a pay phone somewhere. He sounded okay, he's not at risk, and I figured it could wait, or he'd call back. But he never did."

I frowned. "But he did call back, to let you know he was leaving. Really, Malden—"

"Not my cell. He called here, Saturday morning. He knows I don't work on weekends."

"Were there ever specific threats?"

He glanced away. "No."

"No specific threats against any clearly identified individual?" I used words from the law.

Malden shook his head.

"No history of violent behavior, either, as I recall."

"Not that I know of."

I ignored that. "Malden, a patient explores and expresses rage in the safety and privacy of your office. That's nowhere near enough cause for you to break confidentiality and warn these people. Even if you could find them after, what, twenty years?"

"I might have enough." He looked down at the tape recorder between us. "I might have missed something." He paused. "I've been distracted lately."

I stared at this man whose professional judgment I seldom questioned. I don't know if I was more embarrassed or more concerned. Either way, my voice sounded angry, and I meant it to. "There's nothing to hold you accountable for what Robert Percy does."

Malden was up and over at his desk now. "Maybe, maybe not. Things have changed, Sonja. Do some homework."

I responded just as sharply. "Have you considered the damage this could do to Percy's life?"

Malden had no answer. The office was very quiet.

"Malden," I said, "you need help."

"Yes." He looked up. "I do. All I have are the names of a few small towns in central Michigan, and a few families. There have to be files and records somewhere, state or county child protective services, foster care, whatever. I'll try to do more research on the road, but it won't be easy. I'm not sure how much information is sealed. I had Percy sign a release months ago, but it doesn't specify the kind of information I need now." Malden smiled at me, but it was more like a grimace. "I thought, with your connections, you might be able to help."

PERCY

Robert Percy checked the big clock on the station wall, checked his watch, checked the time on his ticket, and checked the small duffle bag tucked between his feet. Two years since he traveled by bus, but he hadn't forgotten how to pack a bag small enough to stay with him, to keep his wallet thin and most of his money elsewhere, and to never lose sight of his ticket. He held it now, tightly in his fingers as if it could blow away or be snatched at any moment, although there was no breeze inside the station and no one seated near him. He wondered why they made them so thin, so flimsy. He frowned. Just holding it was already making it look damp, wrinkled. If the man couldn't read it, they might not let him on the bus. Percy swallowed. He would have to go back to his apartment, go back to work, ask for his time card, make up some story about missing the bus. And the young woman would look sideways at the older one, the one with the cold eyes, and they would smile.

Percy took out his handkerchief, carefully unfolded it, and blew his nose. The air was dusty, smelled like oil and metal, stale popcorn, bathrooms that needed cleaning. He did not plan on using the restroom. He stared at his hands. The color of his skin looked funny under the harsh white lighting. Percy looked away. He hadn't lied to Dr. Malden, not once in all the weeks and months, but there were things he'd left out. Some things he wasn't sure about, and he didn't like it when he confused names and places; it made him worry over how many other things he got wrong. The doctor said it didn't matter, what was more important was what Percy *thought* happened, what it meant to him. But Percy knew the doctor was wrong about that. It was very important to know what was real, what really happened.

Talking to Dr. Malden had helped. His mind was not so crowded now, but other memories had appeared to take up the space, as if now there were room for them. Not just memories, but thoughts about the memories, and then feelings about the thoughts about the memories. Sometimes they all pressed against his eyelids at night, so the next morning he felt weak and tired.

A voice over the loudspeaker garbled something about an arrival or a departure. Percy grabbed his bag and walked to the large glass doors, then had to stand back when they opened, letting in a blast of hot air and a line of passengers, most of them unsmiling, unmet. Then suddenly a girl shrieked and ran, her long hair bouncing, into the arms of a dark-haired boy, and they kissed. At first Percy thought that was nice, until they kept on kissing and kissing and touching each other. He frowned. They shouldn't be doing that. Everyone could see them. It wasn't right. He turned and watched a young woman, her face tired, wheeling a stroller and struggling with a suitcase. The baby in the stroller was red-faced and crying, and the woman was trying to talk to it. Percy wished he could help her, but when she caught his eye, she looked away so quickly he knew not to offer.

Percy was the first to get on the bus. The man looked at his ticket. "All the way to Grand Rapids?" Percy stood there, confused, because he suddenly wasn't sure if that was where he wanted to go, if he had remembered the names right. It had been so long ago, there were so many towns, he had moved so much. But the man motioned him on.

He remembered to take a seat near the front, next to the window; bad things could happen in the back, where the driver couldn't see. Percy watched as people filed down the narrow aisle, slid into seats. Two teenaged girls in tight jeans and even tighter t-shirts stared over his head as they walked past, then he heard them giggling and wondered if it was about him. A woman came on next, turned and yelled at the small boy behind her. The veins in her neck stood out. The boy didn't move, just stared at the driver, the big steering wheel. The woman walked back, and though he couldn't see it, Percy heard the slap.

When she came down the aisle, pulling the boy by the arm, Percy couldn't look at her. The boy's small face was closed, shut tight like a book. His cheek was red. The woman gripped his arm so tightly her knuckles were white, but the boy's face showed nothing, nothing at all.

Percy leaned forward, but they were already past him, settling somewhere in the back, and the driver was closing the doors.

The bus lumbered out of the station into the city traffic. Percy sat back and gazed out the window, but all he could see were her fingernails, dark blood-red, around the boy's small white arm.

2

MALDEN

Joan's apartment was the last stop. She stared at Malden the same way Sonja had, like he was suddenly someone she didn't know. He had tried telling her on the phone, but there was too much to say, and what he'd said sounded unbelievable. It didn't sound much better now, face to face. She made a noise, a kind of incredulous sound in her throat.

"Percy? I thought you were finished with him." They were standing in the small living room, facing each other like fighters or people on a stage, but the more Malden explained, the farther away she seemed.

"This isn't a good time for you to leave, David." Her arms were folded tightly across her chest.

"Don't you think I know that? But he might hurt someone. I'm not sure, of course I'm not sure, but I can't take that chance."

"You take plenty of chances." Her voice scraped at him. "You're taking a big chance I'll still be here when you get back." Joan turned away, toward the window. "Why are you doing this to us? Haven't you done enough?"

Malden snapped back, "I'm not the one who moved out."

Joan spun around. "You think I could have stayed? Are you crazy?" Her face gleamed white, hard. Like armor, he thought, and then right behind that, another thought, much worse, that now this was how she might always look at him.

"I'm sorry, sorry." Malden held up his hand. "I have to go. If Percy left on Saturday, he has a three-day head start. I should be back in a week. I didn't have the mail stopped. There might be things for you." He paused. "Or something from Amy. I already sent her an email, told her I'd be out of town."

There was a silence then, as Amy's name changed the order of things, the words that would have been said next, and next. They stood like that another minute, just the sounds of the traffic below, and the faint voice of a television somewhere else.

"We need to tell her, David. We can't keep this up."

"Don't do this to me." His voice was hoarse. "Not now, please."

She looked away.

"I'll be back soon. I'll stay in touch. You can always get me on my cell." Malden moved toward the door, stopped. "Joan, I'm going alone."

"I don't know whether to believe you or not. How can I?" She asked, her eyes dark, accusing.

"I'll call you," Malden said. At the door, he turned, reached toward her, but Joan pulled back, sharply, as if he meant to hit her.

He walked quickly, long, angry strides down the hallway, hating it all, the shiny walls, textured ceilings, all the doors with their bright new locks, the lobby with rows of mailboxes and doorbells and her name there next to one of them—her name. Then he was outside, letting the heavy door slam behind him.

Malden jerked the car around and sped from the lot, and it wasn't until he was out of the city that he took a deep breath, pulled over on the shoulder, took off his jacket and threw it in the backseat. He stood beside the open door, the wind tugging at him, feeling the intense burst of air when a car hurtled past. After a moment, Malden moved back behind the wheel, but before he pulled onto the highway, he picked out one of the tapes from the pile on the passenger seat. As he accelerated into the line of traffic, the sound of Robert Percy's voice began to fill the car.

Robert Percy didn't start by describing the people, or even what they did to him. He always started with the places, the houses. Where they were, what they looked like, how close in town, how far from town. As if he had to warm up, sneak up on his memories. They did not necessarily come in any order, sometimes jumping from one family to another, from one time to another, which was why Malden finally asked if he could tape the sessions. Of course it was all right with Percy; anything Malden did was all right with him. Malden had realized early on that at some level, Percy was doing this for him, for Malden. Regardless of how often Malden reviewed the goals that Percy had set when they started—Percy's job, Percy's friendships, Percy's future—there were times, Malden suspected, when Percy viewed this as Malden's project, and Percy was flattered to help.

Not all the tapes were devoted to Percy's childhood. Not all sessions ended up dealing with the past, and sometimes, what happened in the homes, those places, didn't come out so easily. Sometimes Robert Percy just sat and cried. Sometimes he wouldn't talk above a whisper, as if the people were standing right outside the door, with raised fists, belts, broom handles. Many times, his statements emerged as questions:

"They were wrong to do that to me, weren't they?"

"I didn't know they were saving that cake. I didn't hear them say I couldn't eat it."

"I only went down the street to play."

"I didn't mean to break it."

"How did I know what that word meant?"

Like a witness in his own defense, he was trying to find himself innocent. When he asked Malden, "Was that so bad?" Malden turned the question back to him. Sometimes Percy couldn't answer, just shook his head. But sometimes he could. "I think they were wrong," he said, or "I was just a kid," or "They had no right to do that."

But when Malden asked him to try to say these things directly to those people, as if they were right there in the office, as if they were sitting in those empty chairs, Percy couldn't speak. He just cried. Malden reminded himself that Percy's survival, never a certain thing, had often depended on his ability to be silent, to say nothing.

It was only when Malden reversed the game, told Percy to sit in the chair and "be" them, that everything changed. The voices that came out of Robert Percy were by turns overbearing, brutal, vicious, demanding, whining, hysterical:

"Come out from under that bed or I'll break your leg. I swear I will."

"See how you like it in there for a few hours."

"I said you can't come with us, and that's final."

"I'll give you something to cry about."

"We don't want you here anymore."

"Why are you always spilling everything?"

"You are so stupid, stupid, stupid."

"Retard."

"I'll show you what happens to little boys who lie."

Percy's face was contorted, his fists tight. Not with his own anger, but theirs. And that's how Robert Percy started to express anger. He borrowed it.

NIELSEN

I did the homework Malden suggested. It had been years since I reviewed the duty-to-warn laws. In the large hospital where I work, layers of administration and supervision, frequent consultations, and clearly defined procedures for evaluating and documenting a patient's risk of harm to self or others were always in place. I had kept up with only the New York state law, which had recently been changed. Whereas before it granted permission to warn, now it mandated a duty to warn.

But I started at the beginning, with the Tarasoff decision of 1976 in California, although I wasn't likely to have forgotten those details. We were in graduate school just ten years later, and the legislation was still the subject of heated debate, at least in the halls of academia. Tanya Tarasoff was the UC Berkeley student killed by a classmate under treatment for depression, and the outcome of the case was a legal duty for therapists to break confidentiality if they learned their patient intended to harm another person. This led to "duty to warn" legislation in some other states; the communications between mental health professionals and their patients, usually protected by law, could be shared when there was a serious threat of violence to others.

In 1981, when Hinckley tried to assassinate Ronald Reagan, a case was brought against Hinckley's psychiatrist; although the allegations were eventually dismissed for lack of a specific threat of violence, the suit was also part of our training.

After three hours of scrolling through articles in legal and psychological journals, I still thought Malden was wrong about his liability in Percy's case, but he was right on one key point—things had changed significantly. Ten years ago, one fourth of the states had no laws addressing the issue; now, only four states lacked some form of legislation, whether by state statute or case law. Although many still limited their laws to granting permission to warn, a majority of the states now mandated the duty to warn.

But there was still no definitive federal law, so the degree of responsibility and the definition of imminent danger varied from state to state. Threats were defined as actual, specific, or explicit; in some states, victims had to be identifiable, or reasonably identifiable, but in others, a perceived threat to the general community or to public health was sufficient. Some states required notification of police in addition to the threatened third party; some did not. And in some, the definition of mental health professional had broadened from psychotherapist, psychiatrist, or psychologist to include counselors, social workers, welfare and social service workers, and even secretaries and support staff employed in mental health settings.

Michigan, like New York, mandated warning "in the event of a threat of physical violence against a reasonably identified third person," with the added condition that the patient must possess the ability to carry out the threat. I doubted that Percy's indistinct rages against his abusers constituted explicit threats against identifiable individuals, but regardless of Malden's liability, a lawsuit alone could damage a reputation, destroy an otherwise successfully career. Absent a good legal defense, of course. I addressed that subject while helping Malden pack up.

"Surely MacAllister has the legal resources in place. More than adequate, I would assume."

He didn't pause.

"Malden?"

"Percy's a part-time temporary worker. His insurance doesn't cover routine therapy. I've been seeing him on my own, after hours."

I didn't ask if Malden had his own insurance. Early years at the hospital, we thought we didn't need it, and now I'm sure he felt even more secure, working in a large private practice. Malden wouldn't spend money he didn't have to. He took the position with MacAllister, not only for more regular hours and better job security, but for the pay, much more than the hospital could offer. Amy's diagnosis, six years ago, had changed everything.

She'd been only fifteen at the time. Malden and I were still working together, so I heard about her depression, her anxiety, the medications that seemed to work but then didn't. Listening to Malden talk about her could be unbearable. He had no defense against what was happening, and he couldn't make a difference. Mistakes crept into his work. The errors were few, and always on the side of too much treatment. He hospitalized a man who was not at risk; he arranged for a complete psychiatric evaluation for a simple, straightforward case of anxiety. The last time this happened with Malden was years before, when his father was diagnosed with a terminal illness. Suffering can make you stupid.

Malden left hospital work a year later, so I had few chances to hear about Amy. When I finally asked how high school was going for her, he seemed startled by the question.

"She's a senior, but I'm not exactly sure how she is. She doesn't talk about it very much with me—with us—anymore. I don't know who her therapist is, I don't know what the treatment plan is, I don't know what meds she's taking. Amy wants to handle it herself now." Malden looked past me for a moment, as if watching something happen elsewhere. "She's eighteen. What can you do?" he said with an unconvincing shrug.

He finished his coffee, checked his watch. "I told her okay, then asked what could I do, how could I help. She said just be a dad." He made a strange face, which I thought about later but never understood.

Two months after that encounter, I got an email from Amy Malden. She wanted to meet with me about a confidential matter and asked that her parents not be informed. I agreed, at least until I knew more. I hadn't seen her since she was twelve or thirteen, a small, thin girl with Malden's pale skin and her mother's dark hair. At eighteen, she was still small, the slight frame and weight of someone much younger, but her eyes looked old, tired.

Amy told me her current therapist was not helpful, that I was recommended by a friend, someone I'd helped, she didn't say who or when. "I want to work with you, but without my father or mother knowing." She paused. "I mean, without them knowing you're the person I'm seeing." She talked quickly, but she looked worn out, as if the flow of blood had slowed, lost its force, retreated deep beneath her skin.

"Why?"

Amy looked at me, her father's look. Why should she say what we both knew? Malden wouldn't be able to stand it.

I changed my question. "In general, then, not about me in particular. I need to know why you stopped sharing information with them."

The look on her face changed, her eyes becoming more uncertain but her jaw suddenly stubborn, resolute. Amy stumbled over her answer, but it was good enough for me. This *was* her business, not Malden's, not Joan's, not mine. It was hers, probably for life—hers to manage. I'd spent weeks and months and years with patients more than twice her age and experience who had yet to discover, or want to discover, that. The least I could do was to help Amy find out if she could.

We had a little more than a year together, but when she left for college, I felt she was ready and I'd heard nothing, in the two years since, to the contrary. Malden's news of her coming home early made me wonder. It's none of my business anymore, but sometimes it's hard to feel that.

PERCY

What Percy didn't remember about riding a bus was how close you had to sit next to someone, how even though you didn't look at their face or arms or hands, you felt the person, heard what they were doing. Percy moved closer to the window, farther away from the guy who slid in next to him at the last stop. The man wore a cap pulled low over his eyes and never once looked at or spoke to Percy, but he might. He might ask where Percy was going, and then he might ask why, and Percy would have to make up another lie.

Whenever he lied, Percy felt guilty, and then sad to be the kind of person who lied. He didn't care as much when it was the people at work, but he still felt bad about lying to Joanne. She was a good neighbor to him. She promised to take care of his cat, though it wasn't really his cat—you weren't allowed to have any pets in the building. The cat came and went as it pleased, through the small window in the bathroom. He wondered if it had a home somewhere but maybe it wasn't a good home, maybe the people were mean to it. Percy kept the window open and left food and water every day, and he called it his cat when he told stories about it at work.

The cat was why Percy had gotten such a late start on Saturday. He had to wait until Joanne woke up; she worked at a restaurant that stayed open late. When she wasn't so tired, she looked pretty, like someone's older sister would look. He didn't have an older sister; foster sisters didn't count. Or maybe he did have an older sister, somewhere, a real one. Joanne didn't talk about her family at all, just about an "ex" she was always mad at. She didn't have boyfriends either, at least not steady ones. He would hear a man's voice behind her door, but not often. Maybe because she didn't use makeup, only lipstick, and her hair was always the same, pulled back tight in a ponytail so her face stuck out, bare and wide. She had a crooked tooth in front; he tried not to stare at it when she talked.

Percy was careful when he talked to her, careful not to talk too much. He knew that turned people off. So he would say "Well, I guess you have to go" or "I'm sure you're busy," and sometimes Joanne would agree and turn away, but other times she said it was okay and they would keep talking. Sometimes he brought her donuts from the shop on the corner.

Joanne thought his cat was funny because it had short legs and dark splotches of brown color on its face. When she found he hadn't named it, she started calling it Homeless. That hurt his feelings—the cat did have a home, his home—but he never said anything to Joanne. They talked about the apartment building, their jobs, the neighbors. Percy never told her anything about what happened to him before.

The sun was low, the light slanting now across farm fields. The bus drove past a large cornfield, the corn standing tall and ready, the ears thick and heavy. Percy knew about cornfields. One of the earliest places was the house in a cornfield. The first time he saw it, when they drove him there, the house wasn't surrounded by corn yet, just dirt stretching out in all directions.

The bare fields were furrowed and rough and hurt his feet. Percy never made it far from the house before they called him back, and he always came back. The corn grew up slowly at first and then faster and faster. He must have been too young for school because he remembered playing in the shade of the corn, the sound of flies and bees, him alone outside, her in the house. Percy couldn't remember what she did in there all day, other than she smoked. It was always safer outside. The corn grew up taller, taller than him, until it surrounded the house like a hedge, and then, almost overnight, it became a thick green wall, closing them off from the other houses, other fields, even most of the sky unless he tilted his head way back and looked straight up. It grew so close to the house, Percy could hear it at night, rustling.

Whenever they left the place, followed the driveway through the corn, and turned onto the highway, the world was suddenly there, wide open, and it made him blink as if he had been living in a cave. Percy tried to hide in the corn once, but they found him and later they told him stories about the creatures that lived in there, ate children.

Percy thought about where he was going. Maybe he should have made some kind of list. He thought about buying a little notebook like the one Dr. Malden had used at first, but then not as often once he started taping their meetings. Percy didn't mind that; he understood the tapes might be helpful, and Percy knew all about confidentiality, knew even before Dr. Malden started to explain it during their first meeting. That must have shown in his face, because the doctor stopped and looked at him carefully.

"Why don't you tell me what you know about confidentiality?"

So Percy told him what he had learned from the social workers and counselors: that if Dr. Malden needed to talk about Percy with another doctor or therapist or counselor, to help him, then he could. Dr. Malden nodded and then asked Percy if he knew other reasons he might have to share information with other people.

Percy nodded. "If I was thinking about suicide or something."

There was a long silence while the doctor observed him. "And how do you know about that, Robert?"

Percy was quick to answer. "A friend. Well, not really a friend, someone I knew, he tried to hurt himself."

"And how about you, Robert? Have you ever thought about it?"

Percy felt his face burn. He blinked, trying to think of what to say.

But then Dr. Malden apologized. "I'm sorry, that was a very personal question. We don't know each other very well yet."

Percy spoke up. "I've never tried anything. Ever."

Dr. Malden smiled. "The only other reason I might have to tell people what you tell me is if I thought you might hurt someone else." He paused. "I would have to try to stop you."

Percy almost laughed at that. He wasn't sure why.

3

Malden's eyes burned. His neck ached. He knew he should stop, planned to outside of Toledo, but then he kept driving through the dark. He finally turned off the tapes; it became harder and harder to listen. Sometimes he had to turn the volume down, while other times he had to strain to hear at all—Percy's voice was so low, as if it were coming from some deep cavern, a dark echo from another world. And his own voice, always startling him. He wasn't sure why.

The taillights ahead looked distant, but Malden came up on them too fast, and suddenly the car was right in front of him. Malden swerved, slammed on the brakes, swearing. Taking the next exit, he drove another five miles on a dark two-lane road before finding a town and a motel with lights still on, a man dozing in front of a television.

The room smelled like Lysol and cigarettes, but Malden was too tired to care. He dropped his bag on the floor, flopped back onto the bed, stared up at the mottled tiles on the ceiling. He woke later, jolting upright as if he had heard someone cry out. Undressing in the dark, he climbed under the covers and slept until the light coming through the window roused him. It was early, barely dawn, but the small office was open, and he brought a styrofoam cup of coffee back to the room, spread out the map and his lists across the bed. The towns were marked with small circles, and next to them he'd written names, sometimes just his best guess. Robert Percy's speech was nearly unintelligible at times.

The last sessions he taped had no names, no locations. They consisted mostly of noises—Percy's fists, pounding the pillows Malden gave him, fists like pile drivers, rising and falling. Percy's feet, hammering the floor, hard and flat, as if he were stomping something into the ground, past rug, past wood, past concrete, deep into the earth, pounding something down to death.

The tape of their last meeting had almost no sound because Percy had been standing in the middle of the room, fists swinging at air—Percy trying to hit something only he could see. For a moment, Malden thought it might be him, and he could still remember his terror, but then it was over; Percy fell back into the chair, his hands covering his face. Malden's voice, shaken, interrupted the silence. "What is it, Robert? Who are you hitting?" Because he thought he had heard something, he asked again, but Percy just shook his head.

Malden opened the motel door, stepped out. The sky had lightened, but the haze made everything look soft, slightly out of focus. Half real, like the names on his list. They could be ghost families in dream places where only Percy still lived.

There wasn't much to see, a gas station across the road and a house next to it, a tall old house with a tired porch, one corner listing as if the weight of the roof had become too much to bear. As he watched, a woman walked out the door and down the steps to the car parked in front. She wore white pants and a white top, but the whites didn't match. Her hair was pushed back with a wide band, which made her look older than she probably was.

She got into the car, lit a cigarette, and sat there, smoking. A young boy in pajama bottoms walked out onto the porch and stood, his thin chest bare, staring at her. They stayed that way, looking at each other, his arms crossed against his thin chest. Finally she opened the window, said something to him. Malden couldn't hear, but she said it twice before the boy turned and went back into the house. The woman started the car and drove away.

Malden took two steps forward before he stopped himself. No reason to think there wasn't an older brother or sister or father in the house, some adult still sleeping; no reason to read anything into what the boy wasn't saying, what his folded arms and unmoving gaze might mean. No reason to believe the boy needed his help. No more reason than to believe Robert Percy needed it.

If Malden started back now, he could be home in seven hours. Walking back into the room, he closed the door, then bent again over his maps.

PERCY

There was nothing to see anymore, but Percy kept his eyes trained on the dark. The bus was quiet now. The man sitting next to him had gotten off at the last stop, but Percy stayed close to the window anyway.

He'd never forgotten about Robbie, but after he'd started talking to Dr. Malden, the memories came back in larger, longer pieces. Sometimes he wondered if they were dreams, not memories. But then the real dreams started, and what happened in them was different, and sometimes he woke up scared, his face wet though he wasn't crying in the dream. In the dreams there was only screaming and yelling. Always yelling.

Right after dreams like that, he couldn't meet with Dr. Malden. He had to call and give some excuse, and then the next time they met, Percy would repeat the excuse, like being kept late at work or something, his face burning like it always did when he lied, and he could tell by the way Dr. Malden listened that he knew it was a lie. But Percy couldn't bring himself to speak about Robbie. Besides, maybe it wasn't true, maybe he remembered it wrong, got it all mixed up—what happened, what never happened, whose fault it was.

The more he remembered, the harder it was not to tell the doctor. He almost did, Thursday night when he woke up, his head filled with it, his throat tight, unable to breathe. He stumbled down the stairs onto the street, to the phone on the corner, called the personal number Dr. Malden had given him. But when it went to voice mail, he just said something about wanting to talk, that's all. He hung up, hurried back to his apartment.

When he rose the next morning, his head still ached, but he knew what he wanted to do, and it wasn't something he could tell the doctor. Before he left for work, he packed his duffle bag and put it by the door. He folded the paper with Dr. Malden's personal number and stuck it back in his wallet, next to the business card for Dr. Malden's office. The least he could do was to call the office, let the doctor know he would be missing his next appointment.

Percy leaned the side of his face against the glass and closed his eyes. He didn't want to sleep, but after a few minutes, he wasn't really on the bus anymore; he was somewhere else. A small place, too small, and it smelled funny, like old things, old shoes. It was crowded with coats and jackets; no one else could fit in there except him. But it was better than outside, the ground so frozen, so hard and stiff, it pushed up against the soles of his shoes, rock-hard, bumpy. So cold outside, so cold it made his eyes water. Much better to be in here, even locked in here, cramped, than out there. It wasn't cold in here, not like the porch. Percy hated the porch, the piles of newspapers, boots, old chairs, nothing to do out there but be cold cold cold, look in the window, press his face against the glass so they wouldn't forget he was there, that they put him out there, locked him out there.

Blow on the glass, make faces on the glass, draw letters on the glass. *Knock, knock.* It's so cold, please let me in, it's so cold out here. The cold is all over me. Don't forget me out here. The cold is all over my face, inside my clothes, my shoes. Please let me in. I'll be good.

But Percy wasn't out on the porch, because he hadn't been so bad this time. In here, it wasn't cold, but it was dark, just a thin line of light under the door. Even if they forgot him in here, it wasn't so bad. Except if he had to go to the bathroom. That and the dark. And it was hard to stretch out. His leg hurt where the man kicked him. Percy was faster at first, but not later. He cried. Big boys don't cry, but Percy did. He couldn't help it.

He hears footsteps coming closer. Maybe they'll open the door. No, they're going the other way. A door slams. It's the big front door. Now there's nothing. Silence, silence, silence. Except Percy. He's crying.

NIELSEN

Why had Malden sounded so upset? Of course patients hid things. Even the nonstop talkers constantly edited, picking and choosing even faster than the words came out. How much truth did you really need, anyway? You could do a lot with a reasonable facsimile. And even if patients did tell all, tell everything, tell exactly, it was still just their version.

I'd always respected secrets, especially the ones you kept close to your heart, even the ones you tried to keep from yourself. Contrary to current belief, many of them didn't hurt anything, being kept, quietly. Some a warm blanket, some a hair shirt; private consolation, private pain. Not everything benefited from the harsh light of day. Secrets were like stones in a field; below them, there were always more, waiting.

Malden obviously believed differently. It seemed the more he thought about what Percy didn't tell him, the more urgent the trip had become. I sat in my office, much older than Malden's, much smaller, and which sounded even noisier after being in his quiet sanctuary—noise from the corridors outside rising and falling, announcements, voices, footsteps echoing down uncarpeted floors. I couldn't make sense of Malden's pursuit, not that I had much hope of that. I'd gotten into this field not because I thought psychology was the answer, any more than medicine is an answer to death. I got into this field because I wanted to live.

I staggered into it, made desperate by my own haggard habits of self-destruction, the slow torture of my brother's falling. His suicide had orphaned me. Afterward, my parents disappeared into a vast cloud of born-again evangelical religion, as if by allowing their son to kill himself, God now deserved all their attention.

Their withdrawal felt like justice, payback for my having left home too soon, for not returning often enough, never visiting long enough, never paying enough attention, though I did try when they finally called and asked me to. But what did they think I knew, just a few years older than he was? What did they suppose I could see? At that age, all I could see was myself. A year later, he was gone in what my parents preferred to call the accident, but I thought I knew better. Either way, he was the boy who fell. Not from grace—toward grace, I hope, if there is such a thing. There was no grace for me, just a series of days and nights without hope, every week dimmer than the one before, until I realized one day I was thinking about tall buildings.

I wasn't converted to psychology; I hated the sessions but recognized them as necessary, like a bitter pill I had to swallow to stay healthy. I didn't like any of the therapists, but I didn't need to. It didn't matter when I saw their weaknesses, their errors, inconsistencies, blind spots; I was determined to recover what was necessary to keep living.

By the time I completed my therapy, I had learned more from them than they imagined. When I went back to college, studying anything else seemed irrelevant. I finished an undergraduate psych program by the time I was twenty and entered graduate studies younger than most other students. Malden was older than most. We were an odd twosome, Malden and I, and not a popular one. Neither of us used alcohol or drugs; I'd had more than enough of both in the months after my brother's death, and Malden was never interested in altering his consciousness, probably sensed it was strange enough already. But our lack of popularity was due to more than that; Malden's detachment was often taken for superiority, my cynicism for hostility. And our classmates were not always wrong.

We went separate ways for a few years before we ended up working at the same hospital, and Malden said he was getting married. I knew he'd been seeing someone on a regular basis and her name was Joan, but I was shocked. We were in line at the cafeteria, and he was searching his pockets for change. Which was good, because he couldn't see the look on my face. Malden was not the kind of man who should marry anyone.

Most of what I knew about Malden was the little I could see, or guess at—not from what he told me. He seemed to live mostly inside himself, and there wasn't much room left for anyone else. Barely enough for me, and I'd always known our friendship endured only because I didn't need or expect much in return. There were days when he existed in a preoccupied state, giving only minimal attention to anything or anyone not a patient. He was not intentionally brusque or indifferent during those times; everyone else, all of us, were simply irrelevant. I feared for this Joan woman, until I saw her one afternoon in the hospital lobby, talking to Malden. Even from across the room, I could see the line of her jaw, the set of her shoulders, the way she held her head. Not proud, just very certain. I remember, then, wondering who had chosen whom.

Three years later, when Malden told me Joan was pregnant, I wondered what kind of father the man would, or wouldn't, be. I didn't expect any revelations from him. Malden never spoke about his married life; why should raising a child be any less private? I'd always been intrigued by that phrase *raising children*, suggestive of agricultural origins, feeding and sheltering passive animals. The reality I'd seen and heard seemed almost the opposite, even for those parents who somehow managed to maintain a distance from the process, hold on to some power over the outcome.

I'd always thought that having a child would be like falling down the rabbit hole, like Alice in the old Wonderland drawing, toppling backward, her hair streaming out behind, unable to see where she's going. But unlike Alice's descent, there was no end, no finish to the fall. It was deeper than love or hate, the connection with the new presence you'd brought into the world. The word *mother* or *father* lasted forever, even after death took the child or the adult child. Even if the relationship crumbled to dust, even if it twisted into violent antipathy or turned the way of willful indifference, it was still there.

Keeping some distance was easier for men, some men, but their efforts to maintain it sometimes pointed even more to the strength of the connection. The toe-tapping impatience of a father, staring past my head as we listened to his wife's tearful narratives about the adolescent now housed in the detox unit. He betrayed himself in his small gestures, his facial mask; underneath, I sensed tremendous effort.

Malden, even in early years, revealed more than he thought he did, or wanted to.

His face was gray with fatigue when Amy was an infant, he and Joan apparently sharing responsibilities, but if anything he was even more alert than usual, probably due to a noticeable increase in coffee consumption. When Amy was a toddler, there were some days he was called away from work. I never knew why, and I usually didn't ask, though once, after I saw him talking to one of the pediatricians in the cafeteria, I asked if Amy was okay.

Malden hesitated, then shrugged. "Probably just growing pains." He grimaced. "Mine."

The biggest change in Malden during those first years was a nearly obsessive attention to time—this from a man usually so absorbed in his work he had to be reminded he wasn't getting overtime. He never neglected his duties, but he was often the first out to the parking lot.

I saw the three of them one afternoon, meeting there, heading across the asphalt. Amy maybe four or five, still chubby-legged, hopping over something on the ground, Joan waiting for her, Malden much farther ahead, still walking until Joan called out. He turned back, and the rest of way, they walked together—Joan and Amy hand in hand, Malden's palm on Amy's shoulder—until they reached the car.

What little I knew about Malden and Joan's parenting I'd glean from the eighteen-year-old Amy, sitting in my office, already a strong-minded young woman, one who had been allowed to grow in that direction, or perhaps had muscled her way toward it.

We never discussed her parents. I had made clear at the outset of our arrangement that if she had issues with them, she would have to work those out with another counselor. Amy had nodded, yes, of course, they weren't the problem anyway. But still, I insisted.

Despite to my agreement to see Amy without her parents' knowledge, I still maintained some boundaries with the Malden family.

4

Malden never knew how Joan found out. Someone must have spotted him leaving the hotel room with the woman that first afternoon, or the next, because after that there wasn't anything to see. It was over. When he'd caught her eye the last day of the conference, across a meeting room, the woman looked as if she no longer knew him, and he was relieved.

The first day, Malden hadn't recognized her; her face was different—older, of course, but different. He hadn't remembered her name either until she told him. Malden had never known her well, but he worked with the doctor she was having an affair with. Not someone Malden knew much about personally, other than he was married.

She now lived and worked somewhere downstate, but they didn't talk about work, or families, and he never knew if she was married or not. A week later, Malden hardly thought about her, her body, the bed. It was as if it never happened, so when Joan confronted him, he was shocked.

"You wanted me to find out," she told him.

"God, no," he said, "I . . ."

"A local conference? Downtown?"

He shook his head, but she spun around, and he was talking to her back, explaining again and again that it was nothing. "I never meant it to be anything," he said, his voice desperate.

She turned to him, furious. "Of course you didn't, not with her. It could never be anything about her. But it must have meant that much to you. To *you*. Can't you see?"

Malden looked across the room, at anything but her face, afraid that she knew even more, that she knew what it had been like. *It wasn't real*, he wanted to tell her, but that was both truth and lie; it was unreal, the strange time of day, the silence of the hotel in mid-afternoon, a clock loud in the silence afterward. How he stepped out of his clothes as if they were another person's, another person's life. The risk, the danger of being found out, that was unreal also, too terrible to think about. But how real—nothing as real—as the rush of feeling when she bent her neck, when they fell back on the bed.

Joan moved out the next day while he was at work. He wondered if she intended it that way, meant for him to come home to find the house full of an odd silence, so that even though her car was gone, he would stand there, briefcase still in his hand, keys still dangling from his fingers, calling her name. Maybe she intended for Malden to walk up the stairs, open the closet, to be confused by all her clothes still hanging. He sat on the edge of the bed, staring at nothing, until finally he rose and went through every pocket of her clothes. He'd made a pile on the coverlet: coins, grocery lists, receipts, ticket stubs, pens, Kleenex. He didn't know what he was looking for, but he kept at it until he was finished.

He fell back on the bed, the small change rolling against him, closed his eyes. He wanted to find something, but of course, there was nothing. He was the one who'd had something to hide, something he hadn't hidden well enough.

"Is this your way of getting even?" Malden gripped the phone.

"I don't know what else to do."

"I thought we were going to counseling. I agreed."

"Yes, I know. We are. It's next week. I told you."

"So what will this do? Tell me. How will this help?"

"Maybe it won't. I don't know. I don't know. I just can't keep living there."

"Joan, I made a terrible mistake. It wasn't about you. It wasn't about us."

"Was it because I'm going back to school now? I'm gone a lot, I'm busy?"

"God, no. I want you to do that; you waited for years. How could you think that?"

"Well then, what is it? Is our sex life too boring for you? You certainly could have fooled me, but what do I know?"

"Stop it, Joan, please."

"Although I admit frequency has been a problem lately."

"Stop it." Malden was nearly shouting. "It was a mistake. It will never happen again. Don't you believe me?"

She was silent a moment. "Yes, actually, I do believe that. But I won't move back in."

"Why?"

"Because you're a stranger to me."

He slammed down the phone and sank back in the chair. In the quiet of the empty house, he felt something cold and heavy fill his chest.

The first counseling session had been strained, almost formal, despite the therapist's efforts and obvious experience. Middle-aged and gray-haired, the woman had been chosen by Joan; all Malden had asked was that the person be outside his professional circle. He listened to the way the therapist presented the process, her voice careful. Malden didn't interrupt until she referred to what happened as an affair.

"Something that happened two times on a weekend is an affair?"

She observed him calmly. "What would you call it, Mr. Malden? Adultery?"

That startled him; the only context he knew for the word was a religious one. But Malden didn't protest. It was somehow a truer description; he had sinned, mindlessly, stupidly. But it was his sin to deal with, his business, not Joan's, certainly not this woman's.

She started to say something, but Malden held up his hand, spoke directly to Joan. "I'm here because this is what you wanted, but I don't know what you want me to say. What can I say? I'm sorry. It was crazy. I was crazy. I can't explain it."

Joan shook her head. "I need to understand this. I can't move back in like it never happened."

Malden kept his eyes on her face. "I love you. You know that. Nothing changes that."

"That's not the issue." She almost cried the words.

Silence then. Finally, the therapist cleared her throat. "What *is* the issue?"

"The issue," Joan said to the woman, "the issue is that after more than twenty-five years of fidelity—and I believe that, I actually do—my husband screwed another woman. I don't care if it happened two times or twenty times or two hundred times. It happened. Even crazy things have reasons, don't they?" Joan addressed the woman, but it was Malden she wheeled to face. "Isn't that what you people are all about?"

PERCY

After midnight the bus made another stop, a station in a small town; just ten minutes, the driver said. Most people stayed on the bus, but Percy was hungry. He stumbled off, blinking in the stark white lights, and headed for a row of vending machines.

Percy tried to hurry, but it always took him too long to choose. He was still pondering the bags of chips, hand full of change, when he felt someone close beside him, so close he jumped. She giggled. Percy stared at the girl, spiked hair, purple lips, black t-shirt small and tight, breasts jutting out at him. She stared right back, mocking his face, making her eyes round and letting her mouth fall open. Percy flushed and backed away, not wanting the chips now, but she followed.

"Hey. Got any spare change?" She didn't look down at his hand, but she didn't need to. She jittered and hopped in front of him, but her face wasn't moving at all, her eyes on him dark, intent.

Percy didn't want to give any money, not to her, her face, her mean little mouth, so he just stood still, trying not to focus on her breasts, but it was hard not to, a tattoo climbing up between the mounds. She saw him looking, and her lips twisted; she moved even closer, arching her back so they stuck out even farther. Percy stepped back quickly, stumbling, and she laughed. He heard more laughing, and he spun in time to see another girl ducking around the corner.

Percy turned back to the first girl, frowning. "You could get into trouble."

"Oh no," the girl squeaked in a false voice. "You going to report me?" She pushed her chest toward him again, her eyes shiny. But then suddenly she ducked, and Percy realized he'd raised his arm. She backed off warily.

His voice came out scratchy, hoarse, apologizing as if he'd actually hit her, but she continued to move away. "Here." Percy held out the change to no one. She was gone. It had been a game, just a game. He knew it.

Percy walked back to the bus with nothing to eat, but he wasn't thinking about food. He sat and fixed his gaze on the seat in front of him, avoiding the window as they pulled out of the station. He didn't want to see her, or her friend. He didn't need to be reminded she was just a kid.

NIELSEN

There can be a price for stepping into a patient's life, though that price can be even steeper if you don't intervene when you should. If your judgment is wrong, however, it may be the patient who pays the cost. I'd read very little about instances where the therapist's decision to warn was in error. No one seemed to want to know the impact on marriages, careers, and families after unnecessary warnings, when the assumed danger amounted to no more than words spoken in anger and frustration.

Even action to prevent patients from harming themselves could result in damaging consequences. This was the case during my first student internship, many years ago, a drug treatment program in an old storefront in a battered section of the city. I was paired with a mentor who was not often available, and the director traveled among three different clinics. Originally set up for heroin addicts who came for methadone, the clinic now dealt with other addictions, mostly cocaine, speed, and hash; back then, no crack cocaine or meth. I had no idea what the building housed before, but there was always an odd metallic smell even the coffee and cigarettes couldn't mask.

Given my student status, not much was expected of me. I sat quietly during group sessions in the large circle of folding chairs and watched men (no women, I'm not sure why) smoke, tap cigarettes into tiny foil ashtrays, sip coffee from styrofoam cups. I did lead some individual sessions, initially supervised by my mentor, a thick-bodied, heavily bearded man who yawned loudly and frequently. He never sat in very long, and soon limited our interaction to brief discussions concerning the patients he assigned to me.

At first there were three, and then only one, Kevin Melton, a man not much older than I, good looks spoiled by eyes that were usually bleary, a mouth that moved constantly, twisting from sad to angry to confused. He seldom spoke during the group sessions, but talked at length during our private meetings. Kevin had overdosed often enough to scare himself into moving back in with his parents, or maybe it was because he had been evicted from his apartment. The latest incident had involved the police and the courts, which mandated treatment. He talked mostly about his depression, his difficult relationship with his parents, his girlfriend who'd left him, his friends who never helped. One day he looked around the room as if seeing it for the first time—the bare floors, the battered chairs, the scratched desktop I sat behind. "I didn't think I'd end up in a place like this so soon."

I never learned how he got my number. My home phone was unlisted; no cell phones then. Patients were given a series of procedures to follow, numbers of people to call if they needed help after hours; the list did not include interns. I came home late one night and found his messages on my voice mail. The background noises suggested a bar. Kevin was either drunk, high, or both, slurring his words. He said something about trying to get better, but it wasn't working out, it never did. The second message was left about half an hour later, no background noises now. His voice echoed like he was in an empty room; he rambled on, most of what he said incoherent. When I called that number, Kevin answered. I started to ask all the correct questions, but he only laughed, told me it was useless, nothing would help. He hung up, and though I called back over and over, he didn't pick up.

I had no way to assess his meaning, evaluate the risk. Kevin had a history of depression, but not of suicidal thoughts or attempts, at least according to his file. I phoned my mentor twice, left messages, paced the floor of my small apartment, waited, hoping for a call, from the mentor, from the patient. Finally I dialed one of the hotline numbers the patients were given and discussed the situation with a tired-voiced woman who told me it was my decision.

We'd been taught to err on the side of caution, and I did. I called the police and gave them the only address I had. Kevin wasn't there when they woke up his parents, leaving them frantic with worry until he eventually stumbled home, drunk and stoned from his night out. They never forgave him, and he never forgave me. I had betrayed him. He never came back to the clinic, and I found out later he'd moved away and cut off all contact with his parents. They blamed me, unloaded their grief and anger in a long letter to me, and to my mentor and the director. My mentor just shrugged. *It happens. You could have been right.* But I wasn't, and I never knew what happened to Kevin, whether he trusted a treatment program again, or whether he finally gave up, and if he had given up, what that meant.

In the years that followed, I'd made judgments that were sound, taken chances with confidentiality that proved to be warranted. Over the years, I'd developed an expertise, a sense for despair, an ear for the pauses that whisper of death, of endings. But I never forgot Kevin Melton, or his parents, and I kept the letter for a long time.

I took my copy of Percy's file home, though home might be too cozy a word for where I live on the eighth floor of a large residential tower in an old section of downtown Buffalo. Built new in the '70s, before developers realized the appeal of older renovated buildings, it looks like a stack of dinner plates ridged with tiny balconies.

I chose it because I could be anonymous, surrounded by hundreds of people but not required to speak or associate with any of them. I never invited visitors, but I kept the small rooms neat, except for the one where I sleep. That's left to itself, crowded and cluttered with everything I need to get me through the night: books, magazines, television, movies, music. Parked high on a shelf that I could see from my bed were my brother's airplanes, remote-controlled pieces of wood, fiberglass, plastic. They were the only things I took from his room after the funeral.

The file was hardly worth Malden's effort to create it. His list was short. Five last names: Grefson, Alberg, Roglend, Grimble, and Deyer, with question marks and alternate spellings for Roglend, Grimble, and Deyer. Four names of towns or villages: Barnesville, Milton, Bartone, and Wyman, not matched with family names. Malden also included a copy of Percy's intake forms, with his answers to questions about family, health, medications—questions I had asked Percy myself last spring. I read Percy's careful printing explaining he sometimes took aspirin to sleep better.

I knew where Percy lived, out on one of the edges of the city before it sprawled into suburbs, an old neighborhood at one time a mix of commercial and residential, now a series of aged apartment buildings above neglected storefronts, most of the activity commuter traffic using a shortcut. After our first meeting, it was dark and snowing again, typical late-February weather, and Percy was walking, so I had offered him a ride home. Not my usual practice, but he wasn't going to be my patient, and I knew enough about him by then. It wasn't so much charity as curiosity.

Percy had given directions nervously, repeating himself. He glanced at me from time to time, but I didn't encourage conversation; it was just a ride. The neighborhood wasn't bad, just bleak, worn out—housing for people who worked or lived without prospects. But I wasted no pity on Percy; the area was better than some my patients endured. Pointing out an old donut shop that could have served in an Edward Hopper scene, Percy said I could drop him at the corner, but I drove to his apartment, a squat, square building of that harsh yellowish-brown brick that never ages. I waited as he stood outside the doorway, searching through his pockets—pants, sweatshirt, jacket—once, twice, three times, his movements starting to convey panic, before he finally found his keys. I drove off quickly before he could turn and thank me again.

I skipped down the page to the next of kin/emergency contact, the Mrs. Helen Johnson that Malden had told me about, alive and well in Willits, Michigan. Her husband had died, Malden said, but that was two years ago. I'd insisted he start his search with her anyway. Someone Percy called "Mom" might know more than Malden ever would about his patient. Not that I told him that; there was no time to discuss mothers and what they know about us, and I wouldn't broach that subject with Malden anyway.

Malden never talked about his mother, and if someone asked, he replied, "She died when I was seventeen." He always said it the same way, like it was the last sentence of a conversation, and there was nothing more to say.

I met his father once, before he died. He wasn't what I expected, though I'm not sure what I did expect—perhaps someone who accounted for the grim cast of Malden's countenance, someone whose manner explained Malden's restless thinking, his difficulty communicating. But this man, much shorter, stouter, wasn't who I'd pictured. The extra weight rounding out his face made his nose and mouth smaller, his eyes narrower. Despite the extra girth, the whole impression was lighter. Lighter than Malden. No shadows; none of the severity I anticipated.

He'd heaved himself quickly out of his chair and walked toward me, his voice and smile soft but not too soft. There were edges, one or two, but for the most part, he'd been worn smooth. He was watchful, alert, and I wondered what he had been like before his wife died.

Whenever Malden spoke of his life with his father, it was always in terms of "before my mother died" or "after my mother died," as if her absence defined most of their relationship.

I went to his funeral, and afterward saw Malden, his wife, and his daughter—Amy was only twelve or thirteen then—in a stiff little row at the back of the church. Malden was shaking hands, thanking people for coming, listening to what they were saying, nodding. But when he turned away at one point, I saw he was devastated. I watched Joan put her hand on his arm for a moment, and I had to avert my eyes, as I usually did when I saw a marriage at work. It was a way of life, marriage—like a way of breathing, feeling—that some people could manage, some couldn't. It helped if you could figure out how to have mercy, not just on your spouse, but on yourself.

5

Clutching his jacket and duffle bag, Percy was the first one off the bus when the driver finally opened the doors. "Grand Rapids," the man repeated loudly as passengers stirred and yawned and rubbed their eyes. Percy had woken up long before, as suddenly as if an alarm went off, and watched as they drove into the city. He had never been to Grand Rapids before, at least that he remembered. This early on a Sunday morning, there wasn't much to see on the mostly empty streets: an old man with a blanket roll, two young guys in dark suits on a corner, a black woman in a white uniform, walking fast.

The big bus station looked old, but the inside had been done up new, clean and shiny, music even. Percy hurried past the snack bar and the little tables and the rows of chairs toward the men's restroom. He hoped it would be empty, and it was, nearly, just two guys at the urinals. Percy kept his head down, all the way to the last stall in the corner, the large one for handicapped people. Percy hoped one wouldn't show up. First he made sure the extra cash was still where he'd hidden it, some buttoned into the leg pocket of his cargo pants, some rolled inside the liner of his duffle bag. He unpacked the small towel and the little package of moist travel towels and cleaned up the best he could, changed his underwear and t-shirt. He heard men coming and going, but by the time he opened the stall door, there was just one guy at the other end. Percy brushed his teeth, combed his hair. It was almost long enough for one of those little pigtails. Percy wasn't sure, but he might like one.

Percy shaved quickly because he never knew how long the battery charge would last, and because now more men were coming in. He packed the razor back in his travel kit, zipped it shut, and carefully wiped off the leather sides. "Hardly ever used," Dad Johnson had said, handing it to him the day Percy moved out. "Not sure if you have a need for it, I never do. Jean gave it to me years ago, but where do we ever go?"

Percy took the smooth bag in his hands and didn't know what to say. By the time he was able to speak, Dad Johnson had left the room. Percy thanked him later, but he just waved it away.

Percy always wondered about her, the daughter, Jean, the girl in the photos—capped and gowned in the picture in the living room, but much younger in the small one above the kitchen sink, a little girl in shorts, standing beside her bicycle, face screwed up against the sun. Jean phoned her parents, but not often, and they never talked very long, maybe because of the long distance, the cost. They took turns talking to her; Dad Johnson always stood at the window; Mom Johnson always sat, looking down at her lap. After the phone call they conversed with each other, not that Percy tried to hear, but sometimes he did. He knew about her job, her apartment, her friends. He knew they sent her money sometimes. Jean came home only once in the four years Percy lived with them. She stopped on her way to somewhere else the weekend he was off at the Christian camp.

Percy had liked the camp, though lots of the kids didn't. He liked being part of a group, doing all the same things together, eating and swimming and playing baseball, even if he was too slow and heavy to be good at the game. He hadn't learned to play things right when he was younger, and now all the rules were confusing.

Percy might have liked the canoeing better if he hadn't always had to sit in the back because he was heaviest, so he had to steer. Sometimes the canoe went around in circles, and the boy in the front would yell at him, call him names. There was lots of praying at the camp, but he didn't mind that. He never thought much about religion, but he didn't approve of the way some of the boys acted when they were supposed to be praying. It wasn't respectful.

By the time Percy got home, Jean had left, and the Johnsons were very quiet, not saying much. They asked him about the camp, but he could tell they were thinking about something else. He finally met Jean years later, at Dad Johnson's funeral. Much older-looking and heavier than he'd imagined, she simply nodded when they were introduced. At the gravesite, Percy stood in the back until Mom Johnson noticed and motioned him forward. When he moved up, Jean turned and looked at him, but without anything on her face, as if she saw no one. He could feel Mom Johnson shaking. She wasn't crying; she was shivering even though the sun was warm and he was sweating inside his suit. Percy tried to listen to what the minister said about Dad Johnson, but all he could think about was Mom Johnson shivering and Jean's face.

The man in the ticket office studied his computer screen. "Where?"

"Orington," Percy repeated, his wallet ready.

"You sure?"

Percy didn't say anything.

The man shook his head. "No such place. Better check the map." He pointed.

The large Michigan map on the wall was filled up with the names of the towns, so many they overlapped each other. The longer he stared, the stranger they looked. Percy started to feel lost. Why couldn't he remember? On the other side of the state, big black letters spelled Detroit, and without thinking Percy traced the roads north from that city, north and then east, until he finally found Willits— Willits and Mom Johnson.

He told people in Buffalo that he was from Willits, as if he'd always lived there with Mom and Dad Johnson in the farmhouse. Dad Johnson had leased out most of the land, but he still grew hay in the field around the house. Percy remembered the first time he saw the place from where he sat in the back of the car, surrounded by groceries.

They had combined trips to town, the shopping first, then the social services office. When one of the bags tilted, oranges spilled all over the seat; Percy scrambled to pick them up, nervous, scared. Mom Johnson looked back and asked him if he liked oranges. He said yes, though he didn't like them a lot, they were just okay. And then she said, "Well, have one." When he hesitated, she said, "We'll all have one," and she reached back. When Percy gave her two, she returned one to him. And for the rest of the way home, they ate oranges. Percy consumed his slowly, putting the pieces of peel carefully back in the bag, watching how she handed sections to her husband—one for her, one for him—and how he would take one of his hands off the wheel each time she reached out with a piece, not even having to glance at it. How they could keep looking out the window ahead of them and share an orange like that.

Percy took a deep breath, examined the map, and picked the nearest town that started with O.

"Olmsten," he told the ticket man.

"You sure now?"

Percy nodded and paid. He wasn't sure at all.

The girl behind the snack bar was skinny and tough-looking, her cap pulled down so he couldn't see her eyes, but she didn't act mad, even when Percy took a long time ordering. He settled himself with his food, his bag between his feet and his jacket on the chair beside him. Percy checked his sandwich carefully, made sure she remembered the cheese, and started to eat. He always ate slowly, one small bite at a time, one chip at a time. At work, some of the guys made fun of him, told him he was like a dog guarding his food, but Percy didn't care. Being teased about food wasn't as bad as other things. It didn't help to care anyway.

MALDEN

Malden wasn't familiar with Michigan, not like he was with the state of New York, or Pennsylvania, where his mother's family lived, or

Ohio, from trips to see Joan's family, the last one two years ago, Amy in the front seat using GPS on her cell phone, showing him how easy it was, how he could do it himself if he had a newer phone. But Malden never bothered.

He should have. Despite his maps and his early start, he got stuck in Detroit morning traffic, and then lost his way trying to bypass the city. The route he ended up taking put Malden nearly a hundred miles farther north and fifty miles farther east than he wanted to be, the last of it on county roads that weren't well marked. By the time he found Willits and the Elmwood Senior Residence, his shirt was damp with sweat and he had wasted more than half a day. But Sonja had a point: "It's the only real name you have."

"The towns are real," he'd replied. "I mapped them."

She just looked at him. "Real person, Malden." He didn't have an answer to that, and he wasn't even sure how the families matched up with the towns, apart from the Grefsons in Barnesville, and Roglends still in Bartone, at least according to internet directories.

The Elmwood Senior Residence resembled a large new apartment building, stickers still on some of the windows. He had driven past empty fields, used farm machinery lined up for sale, and boarded-up storefronts on the main street, but the business of housing the elderly of Willits seemed to be thriving. The large lobby was filled colorful sofas and gleaming little tables; nothing here for the infirm, Malden thought. They lived elsewhere, the ones who nodded in wheelchairs and had to be fed. There was no one at the reception desk. He used his cell phone to inform Helen Johnson he'd arrived.

Robert Percy hadn't said much about the woman, or her husband, only that they had been older, and they were good to him, so Malden wasn't prepared for the tall woman who stepped out of the elevator. Despite the cane and the gray hair, there was nothing old about her long body, and nothing kindly about her face. Her jaw was strong and set, her hair pushed sternly back from her face with a wide band. She wore a dark blue tracksuit with white trim, and a gold cross around her neck.

"I'm Helen Johnson," she said, not smiling.

"David Malden." He stuck out his hand without thinking, and she fumbled, trying to switch her cane from one side to the other. She decided against it, reached out with the opposite hand—an awkward clasp.

She led him to a far corner of the lobby, where a window showed farm fields, waved him to a seat, and lowered herself slowly into the opposite chair. She set the cane carefully against the chair, but it slipped off, and she propped it up again with a quick, almost angry movement. Before Helen Johnson straightened up, Malden noticed her hand shook, slightly but continually.

Malden had his card ready. She studied it carefully. When she handed it back, he asked her to keep it, in case she needed to contact him. "I wrote my cell phone number on the back."

She blinked.

Malden paused, suddenly unsure. He folded his hands, cleared his throat. "Thank you for meeting with me. Robert speaks very highly of you and your husband. I'm sorry about your husband." It was the wrong thing to say; he saw her eyes change. He had intruded, stupidly. She continued to stare at him, alert. She was waiting, Malden realized. Bracing herself, of course. He spoke quickly. "Robert's fine; he's okay. I saw him just last week."

Nothing changed but her shoulders, a slight settling back into the chair.

"Robert left on vacation a few days ago, but I need to find him. Something's come up, something I need to discuss with him. I thought he might have come here, to see you."

Helen Johnson regarded him warily. "Why would you think that?"

"He told some people he was going home," Malden said.

Helen Johnson thought about that for a moment. "Last time he was here was two years ago. For the funeral," she added. "He wanted to stay and help, but I told him he needed to get back to his job." She paused, looked past Malden, out at the field. "There's nothing for him here, no jobs. There never was, after he finished school." Her gaze shifted back to Malden. "He's still working, isn't he?"

"Yes, he is."

She nodded.

Malden leaned forward. "Mrs. Johnson, do you have any idea where he might have gone? Maybe to visit some of the other families, to see the people he lived with before?"

"After the way they treated him?" she snapped. But then she spoke more carefully. "Not that he ever said much about it. We never asked. He was a teenager by then; we respected his privacy. But he cried too much, a big boy that age, still crying." She shook her head. "We put him in the bedroom down the hall, and we could hear him at night. Sometimes he would cry out, and I wanted to go to him, but Jim would never let me. He thought it wasn't safe. Robert was a big boy. Jim thought he might strike out, in his sleep. That was nonsense, of course, but . . ." She shook her head. "Sometimes Jim would get up and stand outside the door, ask if he was okay. He'd wait there until Robert said he was, then he would come back to bed. His feet always cold, those old floors."

Malden watched her eyes. She wasn't really thinking about Robert back then; she was thinking about what Malden had said—thinking about Robert now.

"What did he call out? Do you remember any names?"

The woman was quiet a moment. Then another.

Malden read her hesitation. "I'm not a policeman, you know."

"Of course you're not," she said sharply, causing him to flush. "I'm sorry, but I really don't remember. And I don't know where Robert is. Some of the families lived over near Grand Rapids, but I don't recall where."

She reached down for the cane, pushed herself up from the chair. "He was our boy, you know. For four years. We sat at his high school graduation."

Malden stood, waited until she was steady. "If you hear from him, could you call me, or ask him to call me? I'd really appreciate it."

Helen Johnson tilted her head. "You know, at first I thought you might be his pastor."

The expression on Malden's face must have been funny, because she grinned suddenly, a brief flash of almost mischief, a hint of who she might have been. Before the cane, Malden thought, before the funeral, maybe even before Robert Percy.

"But then I remembered," she said, serious again, "how Robert felt about God. I doubt that changed. Not that you could blame him, going through a childhood like that. What kind of God lets those things happen? Better there wasn't one at all than one like that." She paused. "Still, he came along with us every Sunday—just to please me, I knew that. But I always hoped. I thought it would be such a comfort to him." She held Malden's gaze. "It can be a comfort, you know, believing."

At the elevator, he thanked her again.

"Not much help, was I?" she said. "If you find Robert Percy, you tell him not to take too much vacation time. Tell him to get back to work. It's important to have work."

Malden sat in his car with the map propped on the wheel. Mrs. Johnson hadn't asked him why he was looking for Robert Percy. A very reasonable question . . . why a man in his profession—not a pastor, not a policeman—would go chasing after someone who didn't want him to know where they were going. Maybe Helen Johnson wasn't the kind of woman to pry, but as Malden pulled out of the parking lot and headed back toward the interstate, he wondered if Mrs. Johnson already had a pretty good idea of the answer.

NIELSEN

It wasn't the last time I saw my brother, but the time I remembered most often. I was home from college to visit, my parents' concerns about him grown loud enough for me to finally hear. We sat in his room, without much to say after I asked about school, about friends. I told him a few stories of college life. He sat on the floor, fiddling with a model airplane in his lap, until I asked about it. Remote-controlled, he explained; he called it RC.

I laughed and said, "Like Catholics?" But he didn't think that was funny. Or maybe he didn't get it. When I asked how it worked, he offered to show me down at the lake.

We always called it a lake, but it was more of a large pond. An early spring day, ice and snow gone but still cold, the grass still dead and flattened. We were the only people at the small beach. My brother frowned at the wind, but quicker than I expected, the little plane was airborne, a thin, whining sound bouncing off the water as he made it swoop, turn, nearly skimming the small waves.

I didn't have to talk, which was fine with me; it was enough to just sit on the old bench and watch my brother fly his plane. At sixteen he was still short and small-boned; I'd inherited all the height and breadth. Bird boy, I called him when he was younger. I followed the movement of his shoulders, swaying as if they were part of the remote in his hands. What else can you really control at that age—not much of your life, even less your body.

On the way home, he told me he was saving up for a seaplane that could take off from the water when it was calm enough. I sent him money for it when I got back to school, but nearly a year later, there wasn't one in the collection lined up neatly on the shelf in his room, as if he were coming back. I wondered what made him change his mind. I sat in his room for a long time, but all I thought about was the seaplane, as if it mattered, as if it were an important piece of the puzzle.

I drove out to the place it happened, as if that too could explain something. Not his high school, that long flat modern sprawl of buildings close to our home. The school building from which he fell was much farther distant, an old three-story academy topped in the center with a single tall tower. Built in the early 1900s, according to the plaque on the side of the dun-colored stone, it was a district school until sometime in the '80s. Now it housed only English as a second language classes and occasional community events, though there wasn't much of a community left that I could see. Suburban sprawl had gone in another direction, leaving only older homes, older people, like the ones I saw on porches, finished, families raised, children gone, jobs over.

It had been a long bike ride for him, tiring, especially that late in the day. The classes would have just let out, making entry simple in a flow of people. I imagined him strolling through deserted corridors, or waiting in an empty classroom until the building quieted, cars left. Plenty of summer evening light coming in through the tall windows as he made his way up to the top floor. The doors to the roof and the tower were always locked; the night watchman had seen nothing, heard nothing. He said he never did. The school didn't attract trouble—too far from where kids lived now, partied.

Staring at the small arched openings in the tower, I wondered how he got up that far, and why he'd gone there, so far from his friends—though these were the least of the questions. We were asked many, not just by the police, but by family, friends. We had few answers. He was apparently alone, no evidence of drugs or alcohol, his friends elsewhere; it was not a prank or a dare gone awry. No sign of injury except for what the fall had done. The policemen were tactful, calm, sorry to have to ask: was he troubled by something, upset, depressed? Weren't we all at seventeen? My brother was also funny, sharp-witted, spent time with friends, dated occasionally, and, my mother reminded them, had plans for college. My father sat apart, waiting until after they left to say, "He locked his bike in the rack. Don't they think that's important? He locked it so it would be there for the ride home."

There were other mysteries: how my parents managed to make all the arrangements, how they stayed upright throughout the service, stood and sang in their large new church, more like an auditorium. How they responded to those who came up and spoke, held their hands, embraced them. My brother's friends—four boys, two girls—stayed together, a small island drifting toward the door. Their faces blank, eyes opaque, the shield of youth when the unbelievable or unforgivable happens. I thought about asking them, even approached one boy, but he shied away, and I didn't try again.

6

The bus that left Grand Rapids for Olmsten that Sunday morning was nearly empty, but when it stopped in Jackson, a large group, black people and white people, got on. Most were old, but they were all dressed up—some of the men wore suits, some of the women hats. They filed past Percy, talking and laughing; a few smiled at him. Percy thought it might be nice, going to their church. Mom Johnson's church had been very quiet and serious.

The driver opened the door again to let a short, heavy woman, out of breath, climb up the stairs. She hoisted herself into the seat next to Percy. Up close, she looked even larger. Percy didn't like to call people fat. It wasn't nice. She eyed him briefly before she sat down, but she didn't smile. Her cheeks were full and smooth, like a doll's, but there were wrinkles all around her eyes, and below them, dark shadows that made her look tired.

Percy tried to give her more room, but his shoulder was already pressed against the window, the cold air from the vent blowing up his sleeve. She sat with a bag in her lap, both hands on top of it, facing straight ahead. She wore purple sweatpants that looked fuzzy like they were washed a lot, and thick-soled white shoes.

There was already plenty of room on the floor for her bag, but he moved his feet over anyway. Then Percy sighed, surprising himself. It came out so loud. The woman looked over.

"Sorry," Percy said, as if he had sneezed, and then he felt stupid. "You want to sit next to the window? We could trade."

She didn't answer for so long Percy wondered if he was wrong to ask. Maybe she would complain to the driver. His throat started to tighten.

"That's okay. I'm fine." She waved her hand at what they were passing, trees and fields. "I've seen it all a million times."

She sounded nice. Percy smiled at her. "You make this trip a lot?"

Nodding, she reached into the bag and pulled out a large ball of yarn, two long shiny needles, and a folded square of knitting. She unfolded the square on her lap, patting and smoothing it out. Percy liked the soft colors, pinks and purples, and the pattern, circles inside the squares. "That's really nice," he said.

She nodded again, picked up the needles, and started working. Her fingers, short and stubby, moved quickly, and the needles made soft clicking noises when they touched. Percy hadn't seen that for so long he barely recalled—just a glimpse of a memory, like the edge of something disappearing around a corner.

"Where are you going?" he asked, hoping that wasn't nosy.

She didn't sound bothered when she said, "Visit my grandbaby. First one." She glanced out the window, but her fingers kept moving, in and out, over and under. "My son's baby." She flipped the ball of yarn a little to unwind it. "He and that girl . . . she's still trying to finish school. High school." Her mouth closed in a tight, thin line. "House is always a mess, friends over all the time, beer and junk food." She shook her head.

Percy shook his head too. He didn't know about babies, but he knew the tone in her voice, knew she was right. He knew about houses like that, everything upside down, crazy. He started sweating a little. Percy didn't want to think about little kids in crazy houses. He'd first met Robbie in one of those places; Robbie was two years younger but knew more, knew how to get out of the way, to stay so quiet they almost forgot he was there. He had a soft face that was different on one side. One of his eyes sometimes moved in the wrong direction. You couldn't look at that one; you had to look at the eye that was straight or it made you think he wasn't paying attention. Robbie got slapped for that. He got slapped for a lot of things in that house, but he always laughed. Not out loud, but silently, to himself, smiling, as if it were some joke only he understood. As if the mark on his cheek were funny.

They weren't in that house very long, and when they were transferred, they were moved together. People at the next home called them brothers even though they had different last names. Percy didn't mind that. He'd never had a brother, at least one that he knew about.

The woman asked him where he lived, and after he told her about Buffalo, he asked about her home. She was telling him about her cats when suddenly a man in the back of the bus started laughing, a loud, coarse laugh that Percy knew meant something ugly, something mean, something that shouldn't be laughed about. Percy swallowed, but the woman didn't pause, and neither did her hands. Her fingers kept on working just as smoothly, as easily, as if she hadn't heard. She was right, Percy thought. It was nothing, it meant nothing, and he smiled when she got to a funny part in her story.

When she finished, she asked Percy where he was going, if he was visiting anyone.

"Yes," he said. "My family."

"Special occasion?"

Percy hesitated. "A funeral," he said. "One of my uncles. Tom Guenther." He added quickly, "I didn't know him that well." He didn't want her to feel sorry about it.

She glanced over at him, and he wondered for a moment if she knew. But then she returned her attention to her knitting. "What did he die of?"

Percy watched another cornfield pass, then a row of barns, the new kind, like big metal sheds, glinting in the sun. "An accident," he finally said.

Her fingers stopped. "What happened?" she asked, her voice curious now.

"I'm not sure." Percy thought about Guenther, how he had looked, teeth bared, his arm high, the belt. "I think maybe something fell on him."

The bus stop in Olmsten was just a small two-sided shelter next to a Sugar Creek store. Percy was having doubts even before he saw it; the main street didn't look right. He stepped off the bus anyway, because twenty years was a long time, and things could change a lot.

The heat was a surprise, and so was the wind that snapped and twisted the long banner that hung across the street—words about a festival. Percy wondered if that's where everyone was, but then he remembered it was Sunday. He felt funny being the only person out walking, so he looked into the windows of the buildings he passed, as if he were shopping, even though everything was closed.

He passed old storefronts converted to new businesses: a tai chi studio, a tanning salon, and on the corner a video-rental store with an Out of Business sign, but movie posters still lining the windows. Percy stopped in front of a picture of a woman in a small bikini. He tried not to stare, but he did anyway. There was nothing wrong with looking, but it was stupid, something kids did, laughing and pointing. Some of the guys at work did it, showing each other pictures on their cell phones. When Percy didn't join in, they asked him if he was gay. He just shook his head. They were being disrespectful, but he knew better than to say anything.

Percy liked girls, but he hadn't had a girlfriend until he got to the community college and met Linda Goringe. One day she just sat down next to Percy in the cafeteria and started talking about a band she liked. Linda was skinny on top and big on the bottom, had long hair that she let fall over her face to hide her acne, and she was always biting her nails. She wore t-shirts with names of bands across the front but never went to any concerts. Neither she nor Percy had a car, or much money, so most days they just hung around campus.

One day she told him her mom finally found a job and wouldn't be home all day, and they could walk to her house and hang out there.

Linda knew how to have sex, and if she was surprised that Percy didn't, she never showed it. They didn't have sex very often because her mom worked different shifts and could come home any time. When they were in bed, Linda always wanted the blankets over them, so Percy never really saw much of her naked. What they did was pretty simple and usually quick; in the movies, there was a lot more to it, but Percy didn't comment on that.

Percy was confused about whether they were really boyfriend-girlfriend, or just friends. Before he could figure it out, Linda dropped out of school and said they had to break up because it was too hard to try to meet. Percy thought this wasn't a real reason to break up. He called her once, but she didn't stay on the phone long, and he knew not to try again.

Since he'd moved to Buffalo, he'd had only one date; a guy at work fixed it up, Percy could tell right away the girl didn't like him—the way she talked to her friend all the time and didn't look at him. Percy finally said he had to go, he could walk home, it wasn't far. But it was, and by the time Percy reached his corner he felt so tired he didn't even stop for donuts.

The bank looked familiar, and so did the café with the red awnings. The thrift store with clothes in the window didn't. Percy studied the shirts until he saw himself in the glass. He smoothed down his hair. Maybe he should buy a cap. All the guys he knew wore them, but he thought caps made his ears stick out too much, made him look dumb.

When Percy saw the dentist's office, he figured out why he'd remembered Olmsten. Not because he had lived here, but because they had come here for things, medical things, business things. Percy circled back toward the bus shelter.

It was cool inside the Sugar Creek bus station, and quiet, just a clerk stacking cigarette packs on the shelves behind the counter. He was a thin man, and he worked fast.

"Be right with you." He had a raspy voice, as if he smoked the cigarettes.

"No problem," Percy said. "No hurry." When the man turned around, Percy saw his face was thin too, so narrow his nose looked too big. The name tag on his shirt said Steve.

"Okay, what you got here?" The man was quick on the register.

Percy took his chips and beef sticks over to one of the small orange tables wedged between cases of soda and beer, set his bag down between his feet, and ate his chips, looking out the window. A big pickup truck towing a boat pulled up to the pumps. Percy couldn't remember a lake big enough for a boat that size. The men who came in and bought beer were big too, thick-armed in camo t-shirts. Steve laughed with them, but not loudly. Percy thought he was just being polite.

After they left, Steve called over, "You need anything else?"

"No, no thanks," Percy said.

"There's no more buses today, you know? Not on Sundays."

Percy thought about that, ate another chip.

Steve considered him. "You live around here?"

Percy shook his head. "I thought I lived in this town, but I didn't."

"You looking for your hometown, then. That's cool," Steve said. "Like your roots or something."

"Yeah, I guess."

Steve walked over to the coffee pots and started straightening up cups and lids. "My wife, she's got roots here; her family goes way back. She can show you old graves in the cemetery. I'm from down near Detroit, myself. But I got laid off, and she wanted to move up here, help her mom out. Her dad's gone goofy, you know?"

Percy nodded, though he didn't like it when people made those little circles next to their heads. Some people described that way weren't really crazy, and even if they were, that wasn't the right way to talk about them. But Steve seemed nice, so maybe he didn't mean it like that.

A van pulled up, and Percy watched a woman unbuckle a baby from a carseat. Before she finished, a little boy was already out the other side. Percy couldn't hear what she yelled, but the boy stopped and waited, and they all came in together, the smaller one in her arms, the boy holding her hand. He ran over to the candy bars, squatted to study the bottom row. When she came back with a gallon of milk, he hadn't moved.

"Just one, Davey." The boy picked up a bar, put it back, picked up another, put it back. Finally he stood up, a candy bar in each hand, and she sighed. Percy could see she wasn't mad; she was just tired.

"This for me," the boy said, holding up one, "and this for baby." He held up the other. She laughed and pushed him toward the counter.

His mother would have been like that, Percy thought. They told him he was too young to remember, but sometimes he did have memories—of long, light-colored hair and large soft eyes. He knew she was very sad to have to give him up. Percy never blamed her. She must have gotten pregnant the wrong way, without a husband or maybe with someone else's husband, and she had no way to keep him. He knew she loved him, despite what other kids said—*Not even your mom wanted you.* Percy had told Dr. Malden how hard it was for girls who got stuck this way. There'd been some in his high school, and Percy saw how their families reacted, what the school did, what people said about them, cruel things. His mother was probably just young and in love, had that look girls had when were crazy about a guy—a nothing-to-lose look, an anything-goes look, an all-for-you look. Percy told Dr. Malden he would like to find her one day, but not if it would upset her, or ruin her new life.

When Dr. Malden had asked Percy about his father, if he had any thoughts or memories about his father, Percy shook his head. He had nothing, felt nothing. He didn't even have an idea. How can you have an idea about nothing?

"Like a ghost?" Dr. Malden asked.

Percy had to correct him. Ghosts were what was left after a person was gone. If the person was never there, how could there be a ghost?

When the store was empty again, Percy walked up to the counter to buy a slice of pizza. Steve stuck it in the microwave for him.

"Closest motels are over in Jorgen. That's where I live."

"Jorgen?" It sounded familiar.

"Maybe that's the town you want."

"It could be," Percy said.

Steve checked his watch. "If you don't mind waiting till I get off, you can ride with me."

Steve drove his little car fast. He didn't seem to mind when Percy asked questions about his family, his kids. Percy was careful about asking personal questions. Some people were always allowed to— counselors, social workers, teachers; filling out forms, writing in notebooks—but whenever Percy asked them, people changed the subject, or seemed not to hear. He never meant to be rude. He really wanted to know more about them and their families.

He'd wanted to ask Dr. Malden when he saw the photo on the desk, the woman and the girl in the cap and gown. Percy assumed it was the doctor's wife and daughter, but he didn't ask. Their appointments had just started, and he didn't want to say anything that would screw things up, though he understood almost from the beginning that Dr. Malden probably wouldn't get mad at him; maybe get mad at other people—he had that look—but not at Percy.

The weeks went by, and from where he sat he could see another family picture, a kid's drawing that someone had saved, framed, hung on the wall. He wondered if the kid who drew it was the girl in the photo on the desk.

When Percy finally brought up the picture, it was at a strange time. He'd been sitting with his hands still clenched in his lap, blinking and blinking away the old memories, his throat sore from talking so loud, maybe yelling even; he was never sure afterward. Dr. Malden was still writing something in his notebook, and Percy asked if his daughter had drawn the picture. The doctor hadn't understood at first, and Percy had to point to the wall.

"Oh, yes, she did." Dr. Malden studied the picture as if he hadn't seen it for a while.

"How old was she?"

The doctor hesitated, and Percy realized this was a personal question he had no business asking. But then the doctor put down his notebook and turned his chair so they were both looking at the picture.

"I'm not sure how old she was. Maybe five or six?"

"It's very good," Percy said. "She was good at it."

Dr. Malden didn't say anything, just raised an eyebrow.

"Does she still draw pictures? I mean, is she an artist?"

"No, she studies other people's pictures. She's majoring in art history. She wants to teach."

Percy was still thinking about that when the doctor spoke again. "What do you like about that picture, Robert?"

Since he had been looking at it for weeks, he didn't mind answering. He liked it all, he said: the three stick people, two tall, one much smaller with lots of hair, the tree next to the house, the purple flowers lined up in the front, the bright circle of sun in the corner, the curly smoke coming out of the red chimney on the roof. "Do you still live there?"

There was another awkward pause, and Percy blushed. "I mean, in the house, the one in the picture."

"Yes," Dr. Malden replied finally. "We've lived in the same house ever since she was born."

It was Percy's turn to fall silent. He imagined what it was like to live in the same place, to keep waking up in the same room, looking out the same windows at the flowers and tree. And with the other people, the two big ones, also staying the same.

Percy couldn't tell from the faces—the mouths were red smudges, the eyes just little black dots—but he thought they were happy there. He considered saying that, but by then Dr. Malden had picked up his notebook again, and Percy knew that part of the conversation was over.

Steve dropped Percy off a quarter mile outside of Jorgen, in front of an old motel with a row of blue doors. Next to each door was a white plastic chair, so you could sit outside and watch the highway.

The sun was low but still hot through the windshield, and Malden drove fast, trying to reach Barnesville before it was too late for a stranger to be knocking on a door in a small town. As he approached, he was surprised to find the place much larger than Willits, with heavy traffic on the edge of town, where supermarkets, car lots, and fast-food restaurants lined the highway. Inside Barnesville, however, streets were quiet, and Malden arrived in enough daylight to have no trouble finding the address. The house was small, like most in the old neighborhood, shaded by a long, low roof sloping down over a deep porch. No one answered the door. There was no car in the driveway, but Malden pressed the bell again.

"No one's home." The voice came from the porch next door.

Malden squinted into the shaded overhang. "I'm looking for the Grefson family," he said.

"They moved. Mottsens live there now, nearly three years."

He could barely see the woman in the chair, but her voice sounded old, heavy.

"Are the Grefsons still living around here?"

"Not sure," the woman said after a moment. "They might be. You could check at the town hall. There's a woman there tell you everything about people's business."

Malden was hopeful, but when he arrived at the old brown stone building, a short, stocky man with thick white hair was busy locking up, and told him to come back tomorrow. His suit was rumpled, his eyes tired, but when Malden asked him about motels, he stopped and thought.

"Not many choices around here."

"It doesn't matter," Malden said. "Anything close."

The man raised an eyebrow.

"It doesn't matter," Malden said impatiently.

"Alpine Inn, two miles down." He walked away quickly.

The Alpine Inn was old, set back from the road behind a wide lawn and tall trees, evidence of a Bavarian style still visible in the dark timbers and wooden railings. The room was small, the plumbing dated, but it was clean, and the wireless connection worked. Malden sent off an email to Joan. She hadn't picked up her phone, but he knew she checked mail constantly, in case of Amy. A habit Joan had started five years ago, as if instant communication could have changed anything, prevented the onset of what had driven Amy into their bedroom in the middle of the night, her hair matted flat against her forehead, to tell them she needed help.

"My counselor said if I ever felt this way, I should go to the hospital," she said, looking much younger than fifteen.

Malden couldn't move. He sat on the edge of the bed, trying to make sense of her pale, flat face. Joan was quicker, already at her side.

Amy handed the bottle of pills to Malden. She hadn't taken any, but she had wanted to, and maybe still did. The bottle had no label, but Malden stared at it anyway while Joan talked. She said she would stay with Amy in her room, that Amy could sleep, and they would talk about it in the morning, but then Malden was on his feet, reaching for his clothes.

Amy was silent on the dark drive to Collingsworth. The psychiatric emergency unit hadn't changed much since Malden worked there. He didn't recognize anyone or expect to; four years was a long time when it came to ERs. The staff seemed too young, the lights too bright, letting nothing escape notice—the lines in Joan's face, the shadows under Amy's eyes—and the wait was longer than it should have been for a weeknight.

The psychiatrist who finally came was an older woman—gentle with Amy, and thorough, Malden had to admit. Amy told her the pills were Restoril, but refused to say how she got them. "I told someone I was having trouble sleeping." Amy kept her eyes on the doctor. "It's not her fault."

Given Amy's history, no previous hospitalizations or attempts, the doctor did not insist on admission, but the presence of suicidal ideation, the plan with means at hand, was troubling. There was a bed available, she said, and some time to observe and assess would be help-ful for treatment recommendations. Amy nodded at the same time Joan protested. Malden took Joan's arm, her body rigid next to his.

Outside day was just beginning to dawn. Halfway across the park-ing lot, he noticed Joan was crying as she walked, tears running down her face.

"She's safe now, Joan. They'll work out a treatment plan. Nothing bad can happen to her there." He stopped at the car. "You couldn't watch her every minute."

At home, Malden changed clothes and headed for his daughter's high school to meet with the counselor she apparently had been seeing for months, without telling them.

"Mr. Malden, please sit down." The surprisingly young blond man pointed to a chair.

Malden wouldn't, and so Mr. Garvin stood also, facing him across the desk. Malden's voice was loud, thick with anger as he questioned the man's qualifications, his ethics, his understanding of confidenti-ality.

Garvin listened, blinking his pale eyes, and when Malden finally paused, spoke quietly about the importance of keeping information private for students this age. "Otherwise, they wouldn't tell me any-thing, even the little they can manage. I work hard to maintain the balance, Mr. Malden."

"Didn't they call you? Amy's in Collingsworth."

The man's face stiffened, his eyes growing scared. "She's okay?"

Malden managed a short nod. "She never talked to you about it, about suicide? Wanting to? Trying to?"

Garvin lifted a hand in protest. "I had no idea she felt that way. No idea. Actually, this past month, she seemed to be feeling much better."

"Amy said you told her to go to the hospital."

"I tell that to all students suffering from depression, even mild depression, which was what your daughter appeared to be struggling with. I tell them all that, just in case. Wouldn't you?"

Reaching down, Malden held onto the back of the chair he still wouldn't sit in. Neither he nor Garvin said anything for a moment, then Malden rasped, "She should have told you."

"You think, if I had done better, she would have." It was not a question.

Malden pondered that. "I don't know. Maybe, maybe not. Probably not," he said finally.

The man frowned. "Why not?"

"There's nothing confidential when it comes to suicide, is there? Amy knows that." Releasing his grip on the chair, Malden turned toward the door, finished. "She knew if she told you, you'd have to tell me."

He relayed the exchange to Joan on their way home from Collingsworth that night, after visiting Amy.

Joan interrupted. "Why couldn't Amy come home with us? They said she was stable." She clutched the bag in her lap. Some of the things she brought for Amy were still in there; Malden should have remembered to tell her what was allowed.

"It was her decision. One more night. And the more time they have to evaluate her, the better."

Joan looked out her window.

Malden drove for a while before he spoke again. "The important question is why she couldn't tell me. All this time."

"Us," Joan said, her voice tight.

"What?"

"Tell *us*."

"That's what I meant," Malden said, but for the rest of the drive home, they didn't speak.

After that, Amy did tell them—included them in meetings with the hospital psychiatrist, and then with her new therapist, whom Malden helped her choose. They worked together as she tried different medications, suffered through side effects, had days when she missed school, couldn't eat, occasionally slept too much, but usually couldn't sleep. Malden often stayed up late with her, but it was Joan who would get up early to keep her company, to walk with her around the neighborhood when the sky was barely light, houses still dark.

Joan quit her job to be home when Amy was. "I need to be here for her," she told Malden.

Malden winced. "Will that make a difference?"

"I don't know. But I should have been around more often, when she was feeling so bad." Her mouth was set. "We'll just have to do without the money."

"What Amy has—it won't change because you're here now."

"Of course not. I've read all about that, where it comes from, the brain chemistry. I know it's not my fault. But she was happy, and now she's not. I'm her mother. How can I not think that somehow I was part of it?"

"Oh, Joan."

Her eyes were angry when she replied, "You, with all your experience—all of you people saying it's not parents or schools or friends or environment that make a person so sad. But you're still her father. Underneath it all, you feel it too, don't you? Even sometimes?"

The silence drew out until Malden walked out of the room. He had to, before he said it out loud, before the words choked him. It was enough that he thought them every day, every day, Joan, every goddamn day.

NIELSEN

How Malden and I ended up in bed together twenty years ago wasn't unique or even memorable, but the results were. Nothing happened. You couldn't even say we fizzled out, because for that, you needed a spark first. Malden's expression was puzzled as we lay in the bed like an old married couple, side by side, staring up at the ceiling of his student apartment, the mottled old tiles, the cracked glass fixture, sheets pulled up to our chins, as if now, after rolling and thrashing about naked, we had something to be modest about.

After a while I cleared my throat. "I think I might be gay."

"Well, that explains you." I supposed he was thinking about himself, although with Malden you could never tell.

Then he rolled toward me, serious. "Really, you're gay?"

"I don't know. Maybe. Maybe not." I'd often wondered what it would be like to say that out loud, but it wasn't any kind of relief, not at all liberating, empowering, or clarifying. It was just confusing.

"So," he said, "this was research?"

"No! How could you think that?" After the weeks and months I had watched his face and arms and back, thought about his body, lean but not with a young man's leanness, more compact. In the middle of my protest, I realized Malden was laughing. I slugged him hard, in the shoulder like guys do, buddies, brothers. And then we got out of bed and never got back into it.

All these years later, I still wasn't certain where I belonged. Subsequent attempts at relationships with both men and women hadn't clarified my orientation. What my efforts at intimacy usually confirmed was simply my difficulty with intimacy.

My solution finally was to quit trying, but I had not always abided by this resolution. When Malden reminded me of my connections with Michigan social services, he was talking about someone I preferred to forget. Charlotte Waring and I had parted painfully, though it was not a lengthy liaison. We met at a Detroit conference on child abuse; she was heading up a panel discussion, and I thought her very intelligent, very effective, and, by the end of the workshop, very attractive. We introduced ourselves over the row of coffee urns after the session. It was easy, not because of me, but because of her. Charlotte knew her way; she was sure of herself, of who she was. We spent the next three nights together, and then we spent the next three months and considerable airfare trying a long-distance relationship. She had a large house outside of Detroit, cozy with photos of family and friends, scattered with evidence of hobbies, decorated with travel memorabilia. Whenever Charlotte flew to Buffalo, I rented a cottage for us on Lake Erie; I told her I had a roommate. I suspected she knew that wasn't true, but she never pressed.

It didn't last long, mostly due to me.

"I'm not sure what you're after," she said when I called in the middle of the night the week after cancelling a visit at the last minute.

"I don't know what you're talking about," I lied. I did know, and she knew, and after that, it was only a matter of weeks. Charlotte was the one who called it off, had the sense to. And she had the grace to write me a letter, a kind letter that offered concern and implied forgiveness. I was grateful for that, but it was too simple, being forgiven. I wanted never to speak with her again.

7

Percy was tired, but it was too early to sleep, too much light slitting in between the blinds that wouldn't close all the way. The small air conditioner rattled and shook until he finally turned it off. He'd stayed in a motel once before, back when he moved to Buffalo, but not alone; it was with Ernie, all their stuff crowded into the back of Ernie's old station wagon. This room was smaller, only one bed, but the rest was the same, the frayed carpeting and the worn bedspread.

The last time he'd traveled from Buffalo to Michigan was for the funeral, two years ago. He'd stayed in his old room out on the farm. It was nearly empty; Percy hadn't had much to leave behind. When Mom Johnson told him she was going to sell the place, Percy said he could move back, help her keep it up.

"I won't hear of it," she said.

They sat at the kitchen table where they always sat, Dad Johnson's chair still pulled up to it neatly.

"I already made arrangements," she told him. "I need to be closer to town." But then she looked out across the fields where the line of old willows marked Red Creek, and he wondered if she really wanted to leave.

Percy put his shoes back on, used the small bathroom, smoothed his hair in the spotted mirror, and locked the door behind him. It only took him ten minutes to walk into Jorgen, but even before then, before he saw the houses, Percy recognized where he was, knew without thinking where to cut across the park and follow the gravel road down the hill, past the church parking lot, into the streets lined with small square wooden houses. Cannery houses, they called them, because they were built back when the cornpacking plant was still operating. Percy hadn't lived in that part of town, but he knew other kids who had.

The main street was just as quiet as Olmsten's, all the stores closed, the sun lower now, slanting between the buildings. Something wasn't right; he couldn't find the hospital. Percy stopped and stared at a large white building with a tall steeple. He remembered something about that church, but Robbie wasn't in the memory. This town was before Robbie.

Percy started back, trying not to think about being wrong, how many other things he might be wrong about. He walked fast, his head down, and when he looked up, he was in a different neighborhood; the houses were bigger, older. Percy stopped and surveyed the street. In the fading light, there was no one sitting on a porch or standing in a yard, even if he wanted to ask directions. There was no one but Percy, his heart beating faster, a sinking feeling in his chest.

He started off again, but the street came to a dead end at a rusty chainlink fence surrounding an old brick structure. Percy hooked his fingers through the wire links like he had a million times before. It was his old school. The gate hung open, and weeds grew up through the blacktop, but it was his school. Percy put his face up to a window, but it was boarded up from the inside. It didn't matter. He knew where he was now. He could find his way back, even in the dark.

The bench near the gate was still there, and Percy sat down, watched a car pass by. The next one, a police car, stopped in front of the bench. The window rolled down, revealing a stern face. "No buses here, mister."

Percy swallowed, stood up, and walked over to the car—not too quickly, careful to keep his hands out of his pockets, his arms at his sides. That's what he'd learned . . . he wasn't sure where. It was a long time ago.

The policeman was young, with very short hair and dark, shiny eyes that ran up and down Percy. His arm hung out the window, fingers tapping the side of the car. Percy couldn't see much of the man behind the wheel, but he caught a glimpse of gray hair.

"You live around here?"

"I used to. I was just visiting." Percy's voice sounded funny.

The policeman nodded. "Visiting." He looked at the school, then back at Percy. "Someone said you been walking around, looking in windows."

Percy felt his face flush. "I went to this school," he pointed. "I was in fourth grade here. Miss Mueller's class."

The older man snorted.

The young policeman glanced over. "What?"

"Miss Mueller. You wouldn't know." The older man smiled. "Before your time."

The younger man shifted back to Percy. "You can't sleep here."

"I know." Percy spoke quickly. "I'm staying at a motel. It's called the Oak Grove. He added, "I already checked in."

"We'll give you a ride."

"That's okay. I can walk. Thanks, anyway."

"Get in," the policeman said, and Percy did. It was only a short drive, but he hated it there in the back, and he worried what the lady in the motel office would think. She had looked suspicious when he paid for the room in cash, but Percy didn't carry a credit card. If she saw him in the police car, maybe she wouldn't let him stay.

He was relieved when no one was around, and nothing else happened that night. Percy ate the chips and the candy bars from the Sugar Creek, drank the free soda that Steve had given him, and fell asleep. But something in Jorgen must have reminded him of Robbie, because he had dreams that night. Maybe it was the police car.

MALDEN

He didn't have to wait until the Barnesville town hall opened; Malden learned about the Grefsons the next morning when he asked the old man in the motel office about a phone book.

"The book we got is five years old. No one uses them anymore; we're all supposed to go online nowadays. Hell with that. Who you looking for?"

His directions led Malden to the other end of Barnesville, where newer houses were grouped in gentle circles and young trees lined the sidewalks. Malden sat in his car, staring at the house he'd been directed to, wondering how he was going to do this. On the other side of the street, an older woman watered flowers, but kept her eyes on him. In the light of the late morning, in the quiet of the street, he was out of place. He would have to do something soon or drive away.

Climbing stiffly out of the car, Malden tucked in his shirt—already damp against his back—before he walked up to the house. He hadn't slept well; the men in the next room had come in late, turned up a television loud, talked even louder. It was early dawn, barely light when he heard them leaving, slamming doors, starting up trucks. He pulled aside the drapes to see them go, three men in sweatshirts and denim jackets, coffee cups steaming, no one saying anything.

The young woman who answered the door stayed behind the screen and kept him standing on the steps. Not that he expected anything different—a strange man in a rumpled shirt and wrinkled pants. In gym shorts, t-shirt, and purple flip-flops with rhinestones, she looked too young to have the boy beside her and the smaller child on her hip, but she remembered Robert Percy, barely. She was just four or five back then. She put a hand on the boy's head. She couldn't tell Malden much about her father; he'd left when she was still in grade school.

"No idea," she said when Malden asked where he had moved. "He probably died." She hitched the baby higher on her hip. "Mom might have known, but she passed away last year." The little boy pressed his face against the screen; his nose flattened, his lips stretched out, fish-like, and he started laughing, maybe at the feeling, maybe at Malden. She pulled him back, scolding, which set the baby crying, and that was the end of the conversation, and the end of Barnesville.

Malden's phone didn't ring, but he stopped outside of town to check it anyway. Nothing yet from Sonja, and nothing from Joan—

never anything from Joan. Last night would have been the marriage counseling, and he wondered if she'd gone anyway. Malden had also agreed to individual sessions with the therapist, but after just one, he chose not to continue.

When Joan found out and asked why, he'd shrugged. They were standing in the parking lot after their session.

"She's not my therapist. She's neutral," Joan persisted. "Is there something wrong with her?"

"It doesn't matter, Joan." Malden took out his keys.

"It does matter."

"It doesn't involve you."

"I want to know."

Finally meeting her eyes, Malden said, "She asked me if my . . . infidelity occurred after we found out Amy was coming home."

Joan's eyes widened.

"I was sorry to have to disappoint her. It would have made for a nice, neat interpretation: husband, angry at having to resume burden of disturbed daughter, creates chaos in the marriage."

"Oh, God. David, I never said . . ."

"I know, I know." He sighed. "Have you heard from Amy again?"

"No, not since that last email. I've called, but nothing yet."

"I should have flown over there. I knew it."

"It's only a few weeks more. She said she was getting help."

Not my help, Malden thought. He'd turned to his car before he realized she'd reached out, to touch him, but then it was too late; Joan was getting into her car, her head angled away, and she didn't see him.

Weeks later, it was Joan who finally interrupted the counselor. "Why are you always asking about Amy? We're not just parents. There were years before Amy was born, and there were years before Amy got sick. It was never just *all* about Amy, even when it was about Amy." She sent Malden a searching glance. "It wasn't simple, wasn't easy, but we were a couple."

Malden wanted to say it hadn't always been difficult, that there were good times too, but Joan was right, the hard times were more than hard, especially in the early years, before Amy. What he remembered then was anger—his anger, her anger. Where it all came from, he never understood. Maybe they were angry because they loved each other and were confused by the way it changed them, changed their lives, the way it put them at risk. Those were times when the smallest talk, the most innocent of phrases, could start them cartwheeling, careening down into the depths of their hurt and despair. The only safety lay in silence, so there were some days when they seemed to live without words, thinking hard before saying anything. Nothing was involuntary anymore, and sometimes the bedroom was the quietest place in the house.

Then things eased between them, and then there was Amy. He couldn't recall which came first, and it didn't matter. It seemed to him that the marriage relaxed during that time, shifted into predictable routines, responsibilities, decisions. Maybe it was the parenting, the care and nurturing spilling over into the way they treated each other. He remembered those years as good ones, for the most part comfortable, until Amy was diagnosed. Then, for a time, they seemed to be back where they started, the anger complicated by newer pain.

Six months after her first hospitalization, Amy ended up back in the hospital.

A familiar scenario, then—Malden and Joan walking back to the car, driving home silently, Malden still furious with the psychiatrists. There were two involved now, giving calm, reasoned responses to his accusations about the risks of the new drugs, how they might cause more issues. Risks they were taking anyway.

Once home, Malden sat down at his desk, and Joan went upstairs. He heard her moving around, then nothing. Sometime later, Malden wasn't reading about drug tests; he was staring out at nothing, the sky darkening into brilliant oranges and purples, but seeing none of it. He turned off his laptop and went upstairs. He found her in Amy's room, curled up on the bed, still with her shoes on, the spread pulled over her as if she needed warmth.

"I called the hospital. She's sleeping. We can see her tomorrow."

Joan just moved her hand, a dismissal: *go away, leave me alone.* She didn't need to say it.

And that was what Malden wanted to hear. Misery doesn't really want company; it wants loneliness and isolation, it wants privacy.

Malden backed away, but at the door a wave of sorrow stopped him. It was too much—*this* was too much. He sat on the edge of the bed, took off his shoes, first one, then the other, reached over and removed Joan's sandals, first one, then the other. And then he lay down against her long back, put his arm across her, pulling her against him. She wrapped her hand around his, and then she sighed, or maybe he sighed. It was the sound that he remembered, like a breath held in and finally let go, if only for that time.

NIELSEN

When I heard someone in the waiting room, I thought it was Malden's patient, returning for something she forgot. Or maybe to ask me yet again when Malden was going to be back. It had not been a very satisfactory session. I was standing with the file in my hand as the door opened and Joan Malden walked in.

I almost didn't recognize her. It had been at least three years, maybe more, since one of those fundraising dinners I couldn't ignore. Everything about her looked new, updated, her hair shorter, sharply angled.

She looked confused. "What are you doing here?"

I could have asked her the same, but I was confused myself. "I'm helping with some patients while he's gone. It was easier for them to meet me here."

Joan kept staring at me. At what, I wondered: my cheap haircut, my clothes?

"I saw the light on. I thought maybe David had come back early."

"Not that I've heard." I moved to put the file away, hoping to end the conversation.

"I thought you went with him."

"It's his wild goose chase, not mine." I slammed the file drawer. "Why would you think that?"

Joan didn't answer, but I persisted.

"Did he say something?" I asked.

"No, no." She corrected me quickly. "I see now I was wrong."

I shouldn't have said anything more. What did I owe this woman, anyway, with her fierce looks and her fashionable clothes? Then, on her way to the door, she stumbled slightly, a small, awkward moment, but it was enough.

"Is there something I can do to help?"

Joan stopped but she didn't turn around. "You don't know—about David and me?"

"No," I said.

Her hand went still on the doorknob. "Two months ago. David never told me her name; I never asked. He said it was a mistake, it would never happen again. But then suddenly there's this trip. I don't know what to believe. But it's not you," she said like it was some kind of curious discovery.

I was stunned. Malden?

"Well, he talks about you—you worked together. He admires you," Joan stated flatly.

When I could speak, I surprised myself. "He didn't tell you?"

Her brow furrowed.

"I have a partner," I lied. A double lie. Even if I had one, Malden wouldn't know.

Joan smiled, her mouth bitter. "That never stopped anyone."

"A female partner," I lied again. Not to save Malden; he'd already betrayed himself. But I couldn't bear for her to think it might have been with me.

"I'm sorry," Joan said finally, but I knew she wasn't thinking about me. As she closed the door behind her, I wasn't thinking about her either.

8

Percy knocked twice, then a third time, wondering if Miss Mueller had moved away, or maybe died. Her house was a longer walk than he thought. The morning was still cool, but Percy felt sweat under his arms. He knocked one last time and was shifting his duffel bag to leave when a woman opened the door. She didn't look much like Miss Mueller anymore. She was much older and shorter and very wrinkled, and she was scowling at him, which made her face even more wrinkled.

"Well? What do you want?"

Percy's face burned, and he started talking, but he must have been talking too fast because she looked like she didn't understand. He tried to slow down. "I was in your class at school. Fourth grade. I'm Robert Percy."

She leaned forward, squinting.

Percy said his name again, louder.

She grabbed his elbow and pulled him closer and peered into his face.

"Robert Percy. Robert Percy. Robert Percy." One of her eyes was milky colored, and she smelled funny.

Percy squirmed, but she tightened her grip and gave his arm a shake. "You just give me a moment, young man."

He stood still.

74

After a long minute, she sighed and dropped his arm. "I'm sorry. Are you sure?"

Percy felt as if everything inside him had been hollowed out. He turned his head quickly, but it was too late. He wiped at his eyes.

"Robert Percy!"

"Yes." He nodded and nodded. "That's me. Robert Percy." He beamed.

Patting his shoulder, Miss Mueller said, "Robert Percy. Well, come on in. How did you get so big? How was I supposed to recognize you with all that hair?"

Percy *was* too big for her little house, that was for sure; he kept bumping into furniture as he followed her through a room crowded with chairs and footstools and little tables covered with framed photos. It smelled a little funny, like Miss Mueller, not bad, but like a closet. The kitchen was better, and he sat where she told him at the small round table in the corner.

Miss Mueller offered him tea, which he never drank, but he said yes, and after Percy watched her pour cream and sugar into her cup, he did the same. It wasn't bad. He added more sugar. She made him a peanut butter and jelly sandwich, which took her a long time, but it wasn't bad either, except the bread was a little stale.

She sat down opposite him and watched him eat. "So, why did you come back here, Robert? Are you visiting your family?"

"I don't have family," Percy reminded her. "I lived with the Towsers. I was a foster kid."

Miss Mueller reached over and patted him again. "Of course, of course. I just forgot for a minute. You want more tea?" Before he could answer she stood up and poured him some. "As if anyone could forget Sam Towser. Although we should all try. That man was rotten to the core." She paused with the kettle in her hand. "Sam Towser had a kind of hold on me, from way back. When I was just a girl, I got into some trouble, and Sam's brother had some involvement in this trouble, which I am not going to talk more about because it's nothing for you to know, but Sam knew all about it, and he was always letting me know that, saying if he told the right people in this town my teaching days would be over so fast I wouldn't have time to clean out my desk. I loved teaching, Robert. It was the best thing I ever did, and I sure needed the money. There was my mother to take care of; we lived together till the day she died. It was never very good between us. I hate to say that about my own mother, but she and I never got along, and the older we both got, the worse it was. Like a field of tall sticker bushes between us. You'd think, by then a grown woman, I'd have figured out how to keep quiet, but just one little snide comment from her and I'd be giving it right back, and the next thing you know, the two of us would be snapping at each other like children. She had a very mean streak, my mother. But you know what they say, it takes two." She finally put the kettle back on the stove and sat down.

"Anyway, if it's Sam Towser you came to see, you're too late." She sipped her tea. "He's in the cemetery. His wife moved away right after he died and went to live with her sister in Ohio. For a while one of the sons was still living out there, but I don't know now. You could ask Scotty. He would know. He's my sister's kid. He comes by every week, helps me get my garbage out to the curb."

"I can do that," Percy said. "I'd like to help."

"Well." She smiled. "That might be a nice change for him."

Percy carried the garbage cans out to the curb, and then Miss Mueller decided she wanted to get rid of some old boxes in the garage, and after that she sent him down into the basement for some used-up paint cans.

Percy was bringing another bag out to the sidewalk when a shiny black truck pulled into the driveway, and a man stepped out, glaring at Percy. He was older by at least ten years, bigger around the middle, in coveralls with a name stitched across the pocket. He looked like he could be strong.

Percy started backing up, but Miss Mueller called from the porch, "It's okay, Scotty. He used to be one of my kids."

The man narrowed his eyes at Percy. "I don't remember you."

"I was in fourth grade," Percy explained.

"Scotty," she yelled, "you were long done by then."

"Jesus," Scotty muttered, but he started walking toward her house.

By the time Percy joined them, Miss Mueller had Scotty sitting at the table with a beer and a plate of cookies. She motioned Percy in, pushed him down in front of a glass of milk, and slid the cookie plate over. Percy looked at Scotty's beer and then at his glass of milk.

Scotty examined him. "You go to high school here?"

Percy shook his head. "I was moved," he said. "I went to Willits High."

"Willits? I never heard of Willits."

"It's over near Saginaw." Percy should have stopped there, but he kept talking—about how he went to community college and got a certificate in welding.

"You're a welder?" Scotty squinted at him just like Miss Mueller had.

"Not yet. They didn't have any openings. But sometimes they let me help out after I finish loading and cleaning."

Scotty raised his eyebrows and started to say something, but Miss Mueller cut in quickly. "I was just telling Scotty you were one of those foster kids at Towser's old place."

Scotty took a bite of a cookie, washed it down with some beer. "Nobody out there now, last I heard."

"Maybe since Robert did all your work for you today, you could give him a ride out there just to see."

It was clear that Scotty didn't want to take Percy anywhere. Miss Mueller swatted his arm. "Robert helped me all afternoon."

Percy pushed back in his chair. "That's okay. I got to catch the bus at four."

Two faces turned toward him.

"To Sothee. I think I lived there for a while."

Miss Mueller cocked her head. "I'm not sure you did, Robert."

Percy brushed at some crumbs on the table. He wasn't sure either.

"But what do I know? My memories are all worn out, Robert Percy. Don't listen to me." Miss Mueller gave his arm a little pinch. "You go find out for yourself. Scotty can give you a ride. It's not far, and you can save the bus fare."

"I got business to do today," Scotty protested.

"That's fine," she said. "Robert and I have more business here too. You go ahead, do your business, and then you come right back."

Scotty sighed.

Ten minutes after Scotty left, Percy was still sitting at the table, but with a towel around his neck. He tried to hold very still, but the scissors seemed very close to his eyes, and his skin started to itch. Miss Mueller snipped away as if she didn't notice. Percy hoped she wasn't cutting it too short. He looked stupid with short hair; it made his head look too round and his ears too big. He squirmed.

"Sit still." She cuffed his head. Barely a tap, but he reached up quickly and seized her wrist. She froze, and Percy did too, and for a long moment, everything was dead quiet.

"For Pete's sake, Robert Percy."

He dropped his hand, and she resumed snipping.

After a while, he said, "You always used to say that."

"Well," she replied, "I suppose I did."

Percy smiled.

Scotty's truck was just as clean on the inside as the outside. Percy held his duffel bag in his lap until Scotty told him he could put it in the back. He didn't seem any friendlier, but he thanked Percy for helping his aunt. "She needs looking after, that's for damn sure. She can't remember shit anymore." He glanced sharply at Percy. "I'm surprised she remembered you at all."

Percy thought about that but didn't reply.

"We'll pass the Towser place on our way. We could stop if you want."

"That's okay," Percy said. "I don't need to."

"See if one of the Towsers is still there. You could say hello."

Percy shook his head. "No, it's okay, really. You have things to do."

"No problem at all," Scotty replied, as if Percy had said yes. "How many years you live out there?"

When Percy said he wasn't sure, maybe two or three, Scotty eyed him curiously, but didn't ask anything more.

They drove out of town, past houses Robert Percy didn't remember, but then Scotty turned onto a gravel road he did remember. The drive stretched across a field overgrown with tall grasses and small shrubs. Percy watched the house as they came closer and closer, tires loud on the gravel.

Pulling to a stop, Scotty tapped the horn, but no one came out. The place looked smaller than he recalled. The old shed off the back was gone; maybe that was why. One of the posts holding up the porch roof was missing. Someone had replaced it with a board. There were no cars, no dogs.

Scotty honked again. "Looks like they moved away." All the window blinds were pulled down except one, tilted at a crazy angle. Scotty took off his cap, scratched his head.

"You want to look around?"

Percy stared at the house. "That's okay."

"Suit yourself," Scotty said, opening his door. "I'm going to check anyway."

The porch door was unlocked. Scotty walked inside and waved, beckoning Percy through the row of rusted screens. Percy didn't want to get out. He didn't care what was on the porch, or what he might see if he peered inside the house. Closing his eyes, he saw Mrs. Towser's white face at the window, sorry for him, sorry for herself. What had happened on that porch, in that house, out in that shed, should stay there. If Percy got any closer, it might not. It might come out, come back to him, into his head; he would have to see it again and hear it again, and he wouldn't be able to get away, he would never get away.

"Hey, you okay?" Scotty was back. "You look sick or something." He started the truck. "She probably fed you something spoiled. I keep telling her she's got to clean out that fridge." He swung the truck around and headed down the drive. "Whenever she asks me if I'm hungry, I always tell her I just ate, even if I'm starving."

Sothee wasn't much different than Jorgen, a little smaller maybe, more farms. Percy told Scotty to drop him off anywhere, but Scotty insisted on taking him to a motel. Ever since they'd left the Towser place, Scotty sounded more friendly; maybe he was sorry about Percy feeling sick out there.

He asked Percy why he'd moved to Buffalo, and Percy told him about Ernie, from welding class, whose brother lived in Buffalo and said there were jobs. "His brother said we could stay with him till we got settled, so we went, but there weren't jobs, and his brother's girlfriend didn't want us there." Percy looked out his window. "It was a small house."

He didn't tell Scotty that *he* was the one the girlfriend didn't want there. She said Percy was always looking at her, which wasn't true, but it was hard not to sometimes. She had a big chest and wore low-cut tops. Percy found an apartment in an old brick building on the edge of the city. "I got a job at a Home Depot because I worked at the one in Willits every summer, and I had a good record. But then after a while Ernie called and said they needed somebody at the loading docks."

Scotty didn't ask Percy anything more about Buffalo, or about Sothee, which was good because Percy didn't recognize anything, and by the time they reached the motel, Percy was almost certain he'd never lived there. The sign outside the small green-and-white Pines Motel read No Vacancy. Percy started to say that was okay, he could find something else, but Scotty waved him quiet.

"Something's going on." He turned, and they drove down the main street of Sothee, thick with cars and lined with flags.

"Jesus. This town is always having some frigging celebration." Scotty pointed to a large banner stretched above the street. "Can you read that? They make this stuff up, I swear."

Percy squinted at the sign. All he could read was Days.

Scotty snorted. "Probably Soybean Days." He shook his head and checked his watch.

There was no vacancy at the next motel either, but this time Percy reached for his duffel bag. "I can find a place, really."

"You end up sleeping in a park and get your ass arrested, then what?"

Percy took his hand off the door handle.

Pulling over, Scotty reached for his cell phone as he climbed out of the truck. He walked back and forth as he talked, glancing over at Percy. When he got back in, he told Percy he'd found a place. "Buddy of mine. His mom used to live there. After she left, he tried to rent it but ended up using it himself, for poker parties, hunting season, that kind of thing."

It wasn't far from town—a small mobile home set back from the road on a narrow lot between two farmhouses. Weeds grew up along the front, but the lawn was mowed. Scotty squatted down in front of the steps and came up with a key.

Percy followed him into the dark interior that smelled a little like stale smoke but looked clean. "No bad, not bad," Scotty commented, moved ahead of him, flipping on lights and opening windows, running the water in the sink for a minute. He opened the fridge, saw the six-pack of beer, and told Percy not to drink anything he couldn't replace.

"I wouldn't do that," Percy said.

Scotty showed him where to put the key when he left, reminded him to turn everything off. He pointed over at one of the farmhouses. "They keep an eye on the place. You tell them I fixed it with Jack. They have questions, they can call him." He eyed Percy sternly. "It's just for one night, you know."

"I know," Percy said. He followed Scotty back outside. "I can pay something."

"No need. Just leave it clean."

Scotty paused at the truck. "You want a ride back into town to get something to eat? It's a good two miles. Be dark soon."

"I can walk. I'm used to it. I do it all the time."

An hour later, Percy was still sitting at the small table, fidgeting with the little salt and pepper shakers. He didn't feel like walking. He didn't feel like doing anything. He wasn't even hungry. Maybe he was getting sick. Maybe he should just go home.

The knock made Percy jump. By the time he was on his feet, the door was already opening. The woman who leaned into the trailer was big and wide in a loose sundress, dark hair flat against her forehead, big bare arms hanging down at her sides. Her mouth curved down like it had been pushed there by her cheeks.

Percy rubbed his hands on his pants. "I'm just here for the night," he stammered.

When she didn't say anything, he continued, "Scotty dropped me off. He said it was okay with Jack. I'm Robert Percy."

Her dark eyes didn't show anything, and her voice was flat when she finally spoke. "I called Jack when I saw the truck. I came over to make sure everything was all right."

"It's fine," Percy said. "It's a nice place."

"I did laundry last week. Towels are new. There's clean sheets on the bed." She had a slow way of speaking, as if she was from somewhere farther south.

"I'll sleep on the couch," Percy offered. "I don't want to be any trouble."

With a loose shrug, she said, "Doesn't matter to me. I'll have to change them anyway." She peered into his face. "Jack said you used to live round here?"

"I think I did, when I was little."

Her mouth turned down even more. "I don't recall any family name of Percy around here."

"I was a foster kid."

"Never knew of any folks around here who took in fosters, either." She narrowed her eyes. "Maybe the Roths. Was it them, the Roths?"

"I'm not sure," Percy said. He didn't remember anyone named Roth. "It was a long time ago. I forget things."

"Henry Roth, he died a few years ago, wife before him. Maybe you remember the girl, Cindy. She's a few years older than you, works over at the restaurant near the interstate. She's divorced now but she lives with a man works over at the fertilizer plant in Harwell. You want to call her, you can use our phone."

"Thank you," Percy said, "but I don't think I know her."

"You came all this way, didn't you?" Her eyes pinned him. "Seems you should at least call and find out."

Percy hesitated. "No." His voice came out hoarse, too loud. Rude—he could tell by the look on her face. "I'm not feeling well," he added quickly, which was true. He was sweating, dizzy from her questions.

She raised her eyebrows, but she left. Percy locked the door and watched her walk back to the farmhouse before he pulled the curtain across the window. He wondered if she would call that woman named Cindy Roth, ask if she remembered a boy named Robert Percy. Rummaging in his duffel, he found the can of soda and the bag of cookies from Miss Mueller and sat back down.

The only Cindy he remembered was Cindy Morrow, who went with him to Willits High senior prom. A year older than Percy, she worked in the Bremerton pharmacy and lived with her aunt, Ellen Houghton, a friend of Mom Johnson's.

It was Mom Johnson's idea to put them together, because Percy wasn't going to the prom; the only girl he thought might go with him had said no. He told Mom Johnson it was okay, but she was insistent.

"Did you go to your senior prom?" He wasn't being rude. The question just came out, startling them both.

She blinked, and then she laughed. "No, I didn't. No one asked me. But you should go, Robert. It's the last big event. Graduation is just goodbye."

It wasn't completely a blind date because Percy had seen Cindy a few times before. When he got his learner's permit, Mom Johnson had let him drive her the ten miles to Bremerton so she could visit with Ellen Houghton. The first time he saw Cindy, she was on her way to work—a small, thin girl who looked younger than eighteen. The second time was when he walked down to the pharmacy for something to do because Mom Johnson was still visiting. Wearing a white smock with Rite Aid on the front, Cindy was stacking boxes of toothpaste on a shelf. She kept working while he talked. Her face was pale, and she didn't do much with her hair, which fell flat against her forehead and down the sides of her face in straight lines. Up close, Percy could see she was older; it was something about her eyes, her thin lips. She knew things.

By the time of the prom, Percy had his driver's license; he picked her up at her aunt's house. She looked the same, except for the dress, which seemed a little too big, but maybe it was supposed to, the kind that fell in one smooth line from her shoulders to her knees. Percy thought she looked very nice, and he said that when he handed her the corsage—a wrist one. Mom Johnson had told him that was the safest bet, but it seemed to confuse Cindy. Her aunt had to show her how to wear it.

Percy drove carefully and tried to think of what to say.

"Did you go to your senior prom?"

She shook her head. "I dropped out the end of junior year."

Percy told her there would be kids there from other towns too. He thought she might be worried about that. "Maybe even from Bremerton. You might know them."

"I don't have any friends in Bremerton. I never went to school there."

She didn't say where she did go to school or why she moved to Bremerton and lived with her aunt, so Percy thought he shouldn't ask. He felt better when they walked inside and into the crowd—made up mostly of classmates, but as he'd expected, there were unfamiliar faces from other schools, other towns. Several teachers were there, some parents too, helping out with chairs and tables for the punch and cookies. A few of the kids seemed surprised to see him and looked curiously at Cindy, but nobody stopped to talk except Mrs. Tammer, his English teacher.

Cindy didn't want any punch or food, and she didn't say anything, so Percy was relieved when the music started, even though he didn't like dancing. Out on the crowded floor, no one noticed how he danced, if he did it right or not, and the music was loud so there was no way to talk.

Cindy didn't seem to care if they danced or not, so they did, but when the music changed to a slow song, she walked away and they sat until it changed back. That was fine with Percy. He didn't know how to slow-dance anyway.

They danced more, she drank some punch, Percy ate some food, and then Cindy left for a while to go to the restroom. When she came back, she told Percy there were some girls in the bathroom drinking wine. She looked amused.

Percy frowned at first, but then he thought maybe it *was* kind of funny. They danced more, and when there was a slow one, Cindy excused herself to go to the restroom again. She was gone for so long Percy started to worry. He moved so he could see the doorway. When she finally came out, she was in the middle of a group of three other girls, and she was smiling a little. She started back toward Percy, but they pulled her with them out onto the floor and started dancing. They danced in a group, sometimes singing along, although Cindy didn't, and she didn't dance wild like the others, but Percy could see she was a good dancer. What she did looked right. More girls joined in, and after a few more dances, the group was like its own party, laughing and singing and dancing. Finally some of the guys started to join in, and Percy thought about it, but it seemed fine to just stand and watch them having so much fun, Cindy dancing, her hair bouncing, her cheeks flushed. She looked so pretty.

When Percy went to the men's room, no one was drinking in there. He wouldn't anyway; he was driving. When he came back, the music had stopped, and the group of girls was gone. The band played three more songs before the girls came out to dance again. Cindy was the last one out, and she stumbled against another girl as she walked toward Percy.

The last dance started out fast, but then it changed, and Percy led her over to some chairs where they could watch the couples swaying slowly.

As soon as the car was out of town, she asked him to pull over. Percy edged off the road as far as possible while she fumbled with the door, and then she was out, and he could hear her throwing up. He turned off the headlights to give her some privacy. When she got back in, he handed her the tissues Mom Johnson kept in the glove box and reached for the afghan that was always folded on the backseat. She said she was okay, but she wrapped the afghan around her shoulders, and after a while she quit shivering.

Before they got to Bremerton, Percy stopped at a gas station, and while Cindy went to the restroom, he shopped in the little store. When she got back in the car, he handed her a bottle of Sprite and a small tube of breath mints. "I used to know people who drank a lot," he explained. He'd gotten a Sprite for himself too. Not that he was thirsty, but he thought he should keep her company.

He walked her up to the front door. All the lights were still on downstairs, and she stopped and raised her hand to her mouth.

"Do I smell okay?"

Percy leaned forward while she stood waiting like a small child.

"It's fine." He stepped back. "It's okay. You're fine."

She handed him the afghan, and he stood there for a moment. "Thanks for coming with me."

She stared at him, an odd look, but she didn't say anything. She just nodded.

Percy drank his Sprite on the way home.

When Mom Johnson asked him if he had a good time, Percy said he did, and he wasn't lying. It had felt nice to be there with everyone else, doing something together. And he liked the part where Cindy was dancing and laughing with the other girls. He wondered if maybe that didn't happen much to her. Maybe he should have joined in, but it wouldn't have been the same. He'd even liked taking care of her afterward. He knew how to do that kind of thing, how to help, to not talk or ask stupid questions. Percy never saw her again, but he thought about her sometimes, her thin shoulders, her bare face under the porch light, and he wondered whatever happened to her.

MALDEN

There was no quick route from Barnesville to Milton, just mile after mile of two-lane roads shimmering with heat and crowded with slow-moving farm trucks. For long minutes Malden didn't think about anything but the road, didn't look at anything but what was in front of him, didn't care to notice what he passed, the small towns he drove through. Once he missed a turn and had to backtrack half an hour. He finally stopped, pulled off to get out and stretch, rub his eyes. The wind was hot, pressed the heat through his shirt, and whistled through the old silo across the road, one side broken open to the weather, bricks crumbling around the base. It was all like an odd dream, these roads and fields and towns.

There was no sign announcing Milton; the county road simply became the main street, a mile-long stretch anchored by an old church at one end and a gas station at the other. In between, Malden passed an auto parts store, a small cinderblock post office, a liquor store, two bars, and a diner. Everything old, worn-looking, except for the Dollar General. There wasn't much else to Milton besides a few residential streets that seemed to dead-end after a block.

Malden had no address for the Alberg family. He stopped at the gas station—as old as most of Milton but still busy. Both bay doors were open, and Malden saw a car up on a lift, but there was no one in the small, dusty office that smelled of oil. He waited. A plastic radio blared a talk show; on the other side of the wall, someone hammered on metal. Malden noticed the small adding machine with yellowed keys on the desk, the stained percolator in the corner, like the one in the shop where his father always took their car. Malden had been very young; what interested him most while he waited for his father to finish his conversation was the glass globe filled with gumballs.

It was always a long wait, his father enjoying the discussion, at ease with the men in the coveralls, obviously quite knowledgeable about mechanical details. It was surprising, Malden realized years later, in a man who never worked on cars or made a living with his hands. Malden knew nothing more than necessary about the cars he drove, always took them back to the dealers for repairs, sat in waiting rooms with armchairs, televisions, wireless service, and fresh coffee—far from the sounds and sights of physical labor.

"Hey."

The voice was big, but the man was not; he was small, almost scrawny inside the loose coveralls, his eyes wary. He stood in the doorway, wiping his hands on a rag while Malden asked about the Albergs.

"Never knew them," he said, as if that finished it, but he stayed where he was, wiping his hands. His fingers were thick, knobbed, his gaze fixed on Malden's face.

After a moment, Malden nodded. "Thanks anyway." He made a move toward the door.

"Charlie," the man suddenly called out without turning his head. The hammering stopped. "You know any Albergs around here?"

Silence, then footsteps. Charlie was tall, his head and shoulders visible above his boss, his face curious to see who wanted to know. "There might be some out near the old town line road."

His directions led Malden so far away from Milton that he suspected a joke until he saw the mailbox, and then the name wasn't Alberg, it was Alger. Close enough, Malden thought, though the mobile home looked too new to have housed any family of Percy's memory. He was halfway out of the car when the dogs started for him, two German shepherds on the attack. Malden stood behind the car door and tapped his horn.

The woman who came out didn't call off the dogs. She walked toward the car, the wind blowing her hair and her blouse before she stopped and shaded her eyes with her hand, keeping the dogs between them. She could have been Malden's age, maybe older—old enough to have known Robert Percy.

Malden raised his voice over the barking. "Is this the Alberg home?"

"Alger," she corrected. "No Albergs here."

"I'm looking for someone. Robert Percy. He used to live around here."

"Never heard of him." She dropped her hand and turned to go.

"He used to live with a family named Alberg, or Alger."

She just shook her head and kept walking.

The dogs followed the car down the driveway. Malden checked the rearview mirror when he reached the main road; they were still there, sitting at the edge of the property.

Malden paid attention to the gas gauge but then didn't. When the engine started to sputter, he pulled off the road as far as he could, but the shoulder was narrow, and the ground dropped down into a ditch. Malden punched the emergency flashers on and bent over his map. He looked up when he saw a pickup pass, watched as it stopped and slowly backed up. Not old, but heavily used, metal boxes in the back, long ladders braced on top.

Malden stumbled along the edge of the ditch to greet the man walking toward him, a broad man in jeans and a workshirt. He had a darkly tanned face, a closely trimmed beard going gray.

"You're about fifteen miles from the nearest gas station, maybe twenty-five to any mechanic." The voice was pleasant—not friendly, just efficient.

"Gas," Malden said. "Just gas."

"I can drop you off. They'll drive you back, but depends on who's there. Might be a wait."

Malden locked his car, and stood patiently while the man slid papers and tools off the passenger side.

"Nothing valuable in the car?"

Malden checked for his wallet and his cell phone, shook his head.

They drove in silence. After a few miles the man started looking for something, patting his shirt pockets, and Malden thought it might be cigarettes. The truck smelled faintly of stale smoke. When the man grunted and held up a pack of gum, put two pieces in his mouth, Malden understood.

The man saw him looking. "You ever smoke?"

"Yes," Malden said. "Years."

"Finally beat it?"

"Finally," Malden said.

The man sighed. "It's a son of a bitch."

Malden nodded. "My wife gets the credit." Joan insistent—*We are not raising a child in a house full of smoke*—even though he was already limited to the back porch and the garage. The hospital had been nonsmoking for years, but oddly enough that didn't make quitting any easier, as if, narrowed to small, infrequent releases, the addiction became even more desperate.

"A wife might help," the man agreed. "Maybe I should try one again." He laughed, but it was a short, dry sound not meant to be funny.

The gas station was the only building at the lonely intersection of county roads. The man running the place had to yell twice before a sullen-faced teenager appeared from the back, eyes still on his cell phone. He grabbed keys and the gas can, ignoring Malden as he drove the old car too fast, careless at the wheel, the radio blasting hip-hop at full volume. After a few miles, Malden reached into his wallet.

The kid flicked him a glance. "Dad said no charge for the ride."

Taking out the money anyway, Malden laid it on the dashboard. "It's not for the ride. It's for turning down the music."

The rest of the drive was silent.

After towns like Barnesville and Milton, Eplinger looked like a small city. Malden drove past supermarkets, shopping centers, a golf course with a country club, a cluster of new hotels, and then the college campus that explained it all. Eplinger wasn't on his list, and it was too early to stop driving, but Malden's experience at the Alger house left him unsettled. He couldn't remember if it was Percy who placed the Alberg family in Milton, or whether it had been one of his guesses the night before he left, as he rushed through his notes and tapes. He needed time to check.

The large hotel cost too much, but Malden didn't care; he was hot and tired, and the cool, quiet air of the lobby, the gleaming floors, the promise of a clean room and a desk and a comfortable bed were what he wanted.

"Are you here for the orientation?" The woman at the desk wore horn-rimmed glasses, but the scholarly look ended there. Her blouse was cut low and tight, scattered with sequins that flashed as she handed him the paperwork. When he shook his head, she chatted on. "It starts next week, and this whole town fills up. Three days of activities for parents. They don't just drop the kids off anymore."

Three years ago, he and Joan *had* dropped Amy off. They left right after they carried the last box up to her dorm room. Not that they wanted to; Amy had insisted. It would be easier for her, she said. So they drove away, arrived home three hours later, not talking much, and though it was still light outside, they went upstairs to bed. They had the whole house to themselves, but they made love just as quietly, as carefully, as if Amy were still down the hall.

Malden set up his laptop on the desk, laid out his notes and tapes on one of the beds. The room looked down on an athletic field; in the distance, he could see a cluster of academic buildings. College had been good for Amy, had steadied something in her, and whenever she came home, she spoke confidently about her classes, her room-mates. She did well, but her proposal to go abroad for her junior year had surprised Malden. Joan too, judging from the look on her face as Amy described the program in Madrid, handed them brochures, speaking succinctly, with impressive knowledge.

The only time she faltered was when she talked about the additional costs. She saved some money from her work-study job, she said, but there would be travel expenses. It was an appropriate concern. Though Malden was earning more with MacAllister's practice than he had at the hospital, Joan had only recently gone back to work, and that was just part time.

The money wasn't what concerned Malden, though, and when he said so, Amy had an answer for that too.

"I've discussed this with my doctor and my counselor at college. We made arrangements for services and medications over there, if needed." She stared at him with eyes like Joan's, but their expression was different—unyielding.

Malden was the one who looked away first, down at the papers on the table.

"Dad, I'll be okay."

Joan started to say something, but Amy continued. "You don't need to decide now. You can talk about it."

They waited till much later that night, closer together in the bed than they had been in months, as if this new question had sent them back to the beginning, the years they'd spent lying awake together, listening to each other, wondering where life would take them.

"It's too far away," Joan said. "Anything could happen."

"She thinks she can handle it. Even if it does go wrong."

"Do you think she can?"

"I don't know." He sighed. "When did she get so tough?"

Joan snorted. "Are you kidding? She always was." She rolled onto her side and settled herself for sleep. "She didn't get it from me."

As Joan drifted off, Malden remembered something—something he saw when Amy was arranging the papers and brochures, organizing them into tidy stacks. Her hands were shaking.

The sun was setting over Eplinger when Malden pushed back from the desk and headed for the pizza place across the street. He was sitting in a corner waiting for his order when boys in football uniforms piled in, one after another, loud and rough, jostling each other as if they were still on the field. Too young for college, Malden guessed, even before he saw the high school name on a jacket. He remembered how it felt, the padding and the jersey and the helmet, how they could transform you, how underneath you could be someone else, if only for a while.

The smell, the familiar musky odor of sweaty hair and skin after a hard workout, made Malden wince. He'd played senior year of high school, signed up abruptly late that summer, the summer his mother was dying. He knew about the cancer. He was seventeen; they had to tell him—the options, their decisions, how long it might be. Malden hadn't played since freshman year, which meant he had to learn all over again. He worked hard to catch up, never missed a practice, stayed afterward, until there were just a few of them, playing until the grass was dark and they could hardly see the ball.

His parents encouraged him, sometimes even showed up at practice. They came to the first game, a home game, his mother shrouded in jackets and scarves as if it were cold, and clapped and yelled for him. Three weeks later, she was gone. He would have quit the team then if not for his father—his father sitting in the bleachers, watching.

Malden wasn't rested when he left Eplinger the next morning, but he felt confident. Before he finally turned out the light, he'd sent Joan an email, telling her he was close to finishing; his next stop could be the last. If Percy was after retribution or even just confrontation, he would include a visit to a man named Allen Roglend. Percy had never been specific about what happened, never described any injuries or abuses, but the extent of his rage at the man was significant. When Malden had questioned him, Percy just shook his head, as he often did during his sessions, as if what happened was buried so deeply in his body, it could only find expression in the muscles of arms and clenched fists.

Malden wondered if some of the abuse was sexual, but when he asked, Percy didn't answer, and Malden didn't probe further. A mistake, he thought now. Just because Percy didn't display any of the usual behavior patterns, that didn't mean it hadn't occurred, at least in some form.

He drove through two more small towns, the landscape changing now, fewer fields and more long stretches of woodlands, occasionally a dark, marshy pond. Then the land leveled out into flat stretches without trees, and as he entered Bartone, the town looked flat too, low to the ground, compact—a small downtown surrounded by clusters of older houses. The address from Malden's laptop led him to a small clapboard home, bright white in the sun, lawn mowed so short he could see the contours of the ground beneath. No trees or shrubs, no flowers, but in the middle of the lawn, a tall white flagpole without a flag.

The tall, big-bellied man who answered the door confirmed he was Allen Roglend, his face pleasant until Malden mentioned Robert Percy. Though the man still smiled, everything else changed. Roglend shifted his weight, the large, soft bulk of him moving underneath the thin white shirt. Years ago, the man might not have been so heavy, but he still would have looked big, especially to a boy.

Roglend gazed past Malden at the car, as if he expected Percy to be sitting there.

"I haven't seen him for what—twenty years? Not sure I'd even recognize him now."

"I thought he might have come here," Malden said. "He hasn't?"

The man focused on Malden. "Did he say he was?"

"No. But I know Robert Percy used to live here. I figured he might stop by."

Roglend pulled at his earlobe. "Not sure why he would. He didn't live here long." He looked Malden up and down. "You a cop?"

Malden shook his head.

Roglend leaned against the doorjamb and propped an arm against the opposite side. "Funny little kid, Robert Percy. Not bad; he wasn't a bad one, but he had some bad habits, like a lot of those kids. Not their fault. They pick them up from other people, in those places." He paused. "Percy in some kind of trouble?"

Malden didn't answer.

"I understand you can't say. It wouldn't surprise me. You know, Robert Percy had a tendency to lie. Not just lie, make up stories like they really happened. I think sometimes he thought they really did." He tapped his forehead, rolled his eyes.

Malden thought about Percy pounding, slamming his fists into pillows, sobbing. Whatever had happened to him here was still fresh, still happening.

"Well." The man dropped his arm, pushed his weight off the door. "Sorry I can't help you."

Malden made his way back to the car and sat behind the wheel for a moment, thinking, before walking back to the house and ringing the bell. Roglend was there immediately.

"You said Percy lived in one of 'those places' before here. What did you mean? What kind of place?"

Roglend smiled. "Guess you don't know everything."

"Do you remember the name? Was it a shelter? A youth home?"

"Maybe you should ask Robert Percy."

Malden took a step closer, and Roglend stopped smiling, backed up quickly.

"Was it some kind of institution? Where was it?"

"Don't bother me again," Roglend said, and he closed the door.

This time Malden drove away, fast, his hands tight around the wheel, his face burning. He didn't know if what he'd said to Roglend constituted a warning, and he didn't care. He had no interest in protecting the man. And it appeared to be unnecessary; if Percy, with his three or four day head start, had wanted to contact Roglend, he would have done it by now.

What burned under Malden's skin wasn't just anger, and it kept him driving, not caring where, not thinking about anything except the fact that Roglend, even a man like Roglend, knew more about Robert Percy than he did.

NIELSEN

The message Malden left on my phone sounded different, more urgent, mentioning the possibility of Percy's time in an institution. It wasn't like I hadn't tried investigating Percy's history, but I'd come up against the confidentiality policies that tightly wrapped all the records. I already sent Malden an outline of the legal processes Robert Percy himself would have to go through to read his files, much less someone without Percy's explicit permission. Finding out whether an institution was involved would be impossible.

Unless I resorted to unofficial channels. At my computer, I searched my email for the address of Charlotte Waring and wondered if it was still current. Wondered if, five years later, she still looked the same—wide Slavic face, striking at some angles, strangely flattened at others. A few years older than I, but younger looking, I always thought. Much shorter than I—almost all women were—and slim, but there was something solid about her. She was settled in, at ease with herself, a difference between us that only made me more restless.

The email that popped up was from over a year ago, announcing a change in address, sent out to a long distribution list. It was highly possible Charlotte didn't even remember I was on it.

I started a message, just to see how it would sound. It took me longer than I thought to summarize what I knew about Robert Percy and explain Malden's conclusions. Not that there were many facts; what took time was trying to make the request for confidential information sound reasonable. I'm not sure whether it was Malden or me I was trying to save from embarrassment.

I didn't send it. I saved the draft, closed down the computer, reviewed the list of emergency numbers Malden had left me, and called Joan Malden instead.

I wasn't sure why I wanted to see her, but it didn't take long to find out why she agreed to meet with me. Or maybe that wasn't the reason; maybe it was just the first thing Joan wanted to say. The park, that early on a weekday morning, was quiet, just the sound of our feet on the paved path, so her voice seemed loud.

"I know it was you, working with Amy back then. I found your card in her purse. I was looking for something, anything; she wasn't telling us enough." Joan walked fast, athletic like her outfit, her hands in her pockets, her head bent forward as if she headed into a strong wind. "I hated you for that. I was her mother, but that wasn't enough."

Joan had a different face without makeup—not older or any more approachable, just different. "You don't know how that feels, do you?" She didn't wait for me to answer. "If you did, you never would have agreed to it, behind our backs."

Maybe. Maybe not, I thought. I turned up my collar. I was dressed for the office, not this damp morning.

"I never told David." She didn't say it easily.

"That was good of you." I meant it, knowing how difficult that would have made everything, for all of us.

"It wasn't for your sake."

We walked along for a moment before I asked. "How *is* Amy?"

"I thought *you* could tell *me*."

"I haven't heard from her, not since she graduated. She didn't keep in touch." Which was normal, but in Amy's case, I would have appreciated knowing.

Joan kept her eyes straight ahead. "She's not doing well."

I recalled Amy's face as I'd last seen it, more than two years ago. Not happy, but hopeful. "I'm very sorry," I said.

The pathway curved into a line of trees. I heard the jogger before I saw him, and I dropped back behind Joan to let the man pass, a tall, thin shadow. I had to hurry to catch up with her.

"She's coming home soon, in a few weeks, maybe less. Home to live with us; she said she wants to be back in her own room, just for a while. Great, wonderful, we told her. But that's all we said. She has no idea we're not together."

We were through the trees, out in the open again, heading toward a pond that glinted in the distance. Joan stopped and stared at me. "So what do we do, wait till she gets off the plane? See how bad she's feeling before we tell her? Tell her what? Here's her old room, but it doesn't come with her mother—or here's a new room; it doesn't come with her father?"

I surveyed the long stretch of parkland before us, the road filled now with cars heading for workplaces. I could have been in one of those cars.

We walked back in silence, the pathways busier now with mostly women, mostly older, crisp gray heads, bright sweatshirts and thick shoes, moving along at a rapid pace. Most of them kept talking as they passed, but one gave us a glance, a sharp wrinkled eye; we must have made an odd pair. I don't think Joan saw any of them.

It wasn't until we reached the cars that she asked, "So what did you want to talk about? How shocked you were? How you never thought David Malden was that kind of man?" She rattled her keys. "I can't believe I thought it was you."

I didn't want to know why. I wanted to be finished with this woman and her fierce talk, circling me, looking for something. I turned away, but she continued talking.

"You think I should move back in? Is that why you wanted to see me, to plead his case?"

"I don't know. I might have." I clutched my door handle. "He's my friend."

I didn't expect what Joan said next, her expression almost sad. "David doesn't have any real friends."

I didn't answer her then. I waited until she was inside her car, the door closed, before I spoke. "Neither do I."

I was late for work that morning, but not because of Joan. I stopped at my apartment, walked over to the computer, found the draft message to Charlotte Waring, and pressed the send key.

I had a difficult time concentrating that day. Joan had guessed right: Malden wasn't that kind of man, although I wouldn't have put it quite that way. Any man can be that kind of man; any woman can be that kind of woman. And Malden, no matter how long I'd known him, remained an opaque character.

I was more puzzled than incredulous. Despite our unsuccessful attempt at intimacy so long ago, I'd never doubted the man's physicality, but an extramarital affair was a disruption, an intrusion into an already established life, a foreign body introduced into a system.

Malden's system, I'd always thought, was held in a tenuous balance. A wife and a child were almost too much for Malden.

But that didn't mean he couldn't have been swept away; he was the right age, after all, married long enough for the tedium, the familiarity, to erode the promise of passion. Yet I still couldn't see it. Malden never seemed to relate to women that way. Even before he married, he lacked the requisite awareness of the possibilities of sexual activity. Most of the time, preoccupied with either the work at hand or whatever else was in his head, he wouldn't notice the sidelong look, or the way a voice would change, the spin put on a word or two, but even when he did, he often gave more an impression of surprise than interest, and when he was interested, it seemed to be less about sex and more about the person.

I'd gathered he had experience with women. That was evident during our student attempt to couple. But his was not the expertise of someone who'd had many partners, not the practiced and knowing moves of a man who knew bodies, knew how to get lost, stay lost, for hours in that world.

I'd learned about those men, and women, in the years after my brother's death, when it seemed as if sex might be able to do what drugs and alcohol couldn't. I wasn't virginal even before then. My sexual history started much earlier, accelerated no doubt by my size and my reserved manner; I looked and acted older than my age. At one point I'd entered into an almost wordless liaison with an older boy, one of the few at my school taller than I. I had no illusions of love and no need for romance. The novelty of sex was engrossing and encompassing enough. Charles—his name was Charles, the kind of boy who would never be called anything easier—lived with his parents in a fine old Craftsman house with a separate garage behind it. Above the garage was a small apartment, just a bedroom and a bathroom, built long before his family bought the house. The room was used for storage—stacks of cardboard boxes, lamps, some old chairs—the window covered by a faded curtain so the light was always dim. No bed, but we used the old futon, one of the original models with a wooden frame that banged against the wall. Never loudly; he was a cautious boy, always listening for car tires in the driveway.

We managed to figure out what we didn't know, like learning a new language by feel and touch. I still think of sex that way, as a language. Sex as something conveyed, expressed, many different ways: tenderly, quickly, harshly, impatiently, timidly, resentfully, stupidly, gratefully, automatically. But maybe, after long years of marriage, never just simply.

9

There was no bus station in Sothee. "You have to go to Florin for that," the girl at the diner said, handing him the bag of donuts. She looked like his neighbor Joanne, except for all the makeup around her eyes like a party, and the long earrings turning and glittering when she handed him his change.

"Florin's five miles that way." She pointed.

Percy was used to walking, but after half an hour, he was hot and tired. Flies buzzed around his head, and the pavement ahead shimmered as far as he could see. It wasn't easy terrain; the shoulder of the road was often broken up, choked with weeds. He kept switching the duffle bag from one hand to the other, but his arms still ached.

He didn't plan to hitchhike, but when he heard a car, he spun and stuck out his thumb. It was a woman, driving alone. She didn't look at him, and she didn't stop. She shouldn't, of course. That could be dangerous.

Mom Johnson had made him promise he would never hitchhike again. Percy was in high school, just fifteen, when Scott Forman asked him to come over after school, so instead of taking the bus home, he'd walked to Scott's house—only he never found Scott's house, or maybe Scott mixed up the directions. By the time Percy gave up and started home, it was getting dark, and he tried hitching a ride. No one stopped, but someone who passed must have called Mom Johnson, because she was waiting for him on the porch. It was too dark to see much of her face, but that was the only time, in all the years he lived there, that she'd looked like she wanted to hit him.

He wondered what Mom Johnson would think now, if she knew where he was.

He was still thinking about that when a car of teenagers sped past, yelling at him, the words not clear, but he could guess. After that, he kept his arm down and just walked. It took a while for him to realize there was a car behind him, moving slow.

"Where you headed?" Wraparound sunglasses covered the man's eyes, but the rest of the round, freckled face looked friendly enough.

"Florin," Percy replied. "I'm going to Florin."

The man told him to put his bag in the back, but the station wagon looked full already, mostly boxes.

"That's okay," Percy said, wedging his bag down near his feet.

The man drove with one arm out the open window, the sleeves of his white shirt rolled up to his elbows. His arms and hands were as heavily freckled as his face. He drove slowly, so slowly two cars passed them; the last driver honked and yelled.

"Hot day for walking." The man tilted his head at Percy. "Car broke down?"

"No. There's no buses from Sothee," Percy explained.

"You must not live around here."

It wasn't really a question, but Percy acted like it was. "I used to, when I was a kid."

"When you were a kid." The man laughed. "But you're big now, aren't you?" He looked Percy over.

"It's hot in this car." The man laughed again. In places, his shirt was wet, his skin showing pink through the thin white fabric. "See how hot I am?" He pointed to his crotch.

Percy didn't need to look. He already knew—the cold dread and fear already spreading up his chest. From the stories other kids told, he had been lucky. Or maybe it wasn't luck; maybe he'd just been quicker to fear, to find ways to hide, to disappear. There had been attempts, more than a few, and those stayed with Percy, never left. Squeezing his eyes shut, Percy clenched his hands into fists.

The car stopped suddenly. Opening his eyes, Percy saw the man gaping at him, drops of sweat covering his forehead. He looked scared.

Of him, Percy realized. Afraid of Robert Percy. It was crazy. Percy started laughing.

The man glared, his face red. "What's so funny?"

Percy stopped laughing. "I'm sorry," he said. He opened the car door, grabbed his bag. "I'm sorry, I'm not gay."

"Who's gay?" The man snarled and sped off, tires spinning in the gravel.

The first bus that stopped in front of the small bus shelter in Florin was headed to Worthington, and Percy got on like he recognized the name. He didn't, but when the bus rattled over a set of railroad tracks and passed a trio of tall silos, he hunched forward in his seat. He knew the park, and the big stone church on the corner—not that anyone ever took Robert Percy or little Robbie Duncan inside. Everything looked the same, but in a different way. "I used to live here," Percy told the driver. "I lived here with my brother."

"Is that so?" The man was busy parking the bus in front of the big white courthouse. Percy let two women with large bags, an older man in a white uniform, and a guy with headphones get off first; he was feeling strange, shaky. He stood on the sidewalk, trying to decide which way to go.

"Hey, you forgot your bag." The driver slung it down the steps and walked down after it. He was short, brown-skinned, with wide shoulders and a belly that pushed out the front of his shirt.

"You got to be more careful," he chided.

Percy flushed and picked up his bag.

"You staying with family?"

Percy shook his head.

"Where you staying, then? There's no places downtown anymore.

You got to go two, maybe three miles. There's motels out toward the mall. That way." He pointed.

Percy turned.

"Hold on. I didn't say you had to go all the way out there. You could stay at the Y. Just up the street. YMCA. They have rooms, but no drinking. You know, holy rollers. Go on." He gestured. "Take a right at the corner, one block up. Old gray stone building."

Percy hesitated.

"Go ahead," the driver insisted.

Percy went.

The outside of the building looked old, some of the gray stones stained with rust below the windows, but the inside was much different—bright yellow walls lined with posters and signs about dance classes and exercise programs. A circle of small children sat cross-legged in a corner, listening to a woman read a book.

Percy walked to the counter in the center of the room, where a young bearded man told him they had overnight accommodations, for a three-night limit.

When Percy didn't respond, the man leaned in and asked quietly, "Do you need financial assistance?"

Percy felt his cheeks redden. It wasn't about the cost, not at thirty dollars a night. "I have money, but I'm not sure how long I'm staying."

"Pay one night at a time," the man suggested.

Digging into his reserve cash, Percy paid for two nights.

"There's coffee and tea in the morning, and we lock up at night around ten."

Percy followed the man down a hallway lined with posters of families swimming, hiking, reading, picnicking—everyone smiling, happy to be together. Percy wondered if they were real families, or if they were just acting for the photos. After two flights of stairs, they stopped at a small room just big enough for the bed, chair, and the sink in the corner.

"Bathrooms and showers down the hall," the man told him, "but you're the only one here." He handed him towels and a key before he left. Percy set his bag on the bed and sat in the chair. He didn't mind the little room, the crucifix above the bed. Mom Johnson had always prayed a lot. Percy waited a while before he headed downstairs. He didn't want to follow the man right back down.

The weather had changed, the air cooler, the clouds lower. The walk was shorter than he thought—not that far out of town, past what used to be a car lot, now just empty pavement; past the two fields, one filled now with tall grasses and small shrubs. Past the large farmhouse now painted green, and there it was: the driveway, the mailbox. But the name wasn't Guenther anymore. It was Agio.

Weeds still poked up through the gravel. He remembered Mrs. Guenther going on and on about getting it paved, her face pulled down in deep lines, not happy, not like when she looked at Robbie. She'd liked Robbie, liked him best; she was always patting his head, and she never did that to Percy, even when he was good. Percy always tried to be good. Robbie didn't; he was always forgetting to close the screen door or flush the toilet or put his clothes where they belonged, but Mrs. Guenther never yelled at Robbie, and whenever she made cookies or cake, she let Robbie have the bowl. She was always telling Robbie how smart he was, just because he did better in school, bringing home papers that read Very very good! or Excellent!

Percy peered at the house, which was harder to see now behind the trees. It wasn't yellow anymore. It was kind of brown, and it looked darker, smaller. There were no cars in the drive. As he approached the house, Percy stopped to listen, but there was nothing, no voices, no barking. His shoes were loud on the wooden porch, and when he rang the bell, he could hear it inside. He put his face up against the window, but all he could see was his own reflection.

Around the back, the grass grew even higher, and instead of the walnut tree there was a big stump. The garage was closed up, but Percy didn't need to look in. He knew what it was like inside—dark and damp, smelling like oil and gas and garbage, no place to sit that wasn't hard. He remembered Robbie's face peering in the only window; Robbie trying to make him feel better about being shut inside.

Like a dog, he could have told Dr. Malden. *Like you lock up a dog when you can't trust it.*

Pushing his way through the bushes behind the garage, he found the trail, nearly overgrown; maybe only animals used it now. A minute later Percy stood in the open space of the old gravel pit, the sides of red dirt sloping up, spotted with clumps of weeds and bushes, the ones that smelled like licorice.

It had been Robbie's favorite place. He liked piling up dirt and pushing the little trucks around, blowing out his cheeks, making noises. Little kid stuff, fine for a seven-year-old, but Percy was almost eleven. Once he laughed at Robbie, and he must have laughed too long or loud, because Robbie threw the truck right in Percy's face. It was just plastic and it didn't hurt that much, but Percy cried anyway. That night Robbie wouldn't look at him, but later, in the bunk beds, Robbie asked him if he wanted to come up top and play Pirates. It was another one of Robbie's favorite games—acting like he was steering a big wheel and bouncing up and down as though waves were tossing them around. They played for a long time that night, and before they finished, Robbie let him be captain.

Percy scanned the flat gray sky and listened to the wind in the dry grass, a truck in the distance, crows somewhere. He cupped his hands around his mouth and called. Robbie's name bounced off the red dirt. He called again, louder, and then waited until the sound disappeared before he wiped his eyes and started back toward the house.

When he was back at the garage, he heard tires on the gravel drive. He ran back into the bushes and crouched down, his heart pounding. Car doors slammed, and there was a woman's voice. He held his breath till he heard the front door close, then he ran back to the gravel pit and scrambled up the side, sliding on the loose dirt until he was finally up and over the top. He hurried across the old field, stumbling through clumps of thick brambles and tall thistles that caught at his jeans.

Back at the highway, Percy walked fast, his head down, so he didn't see the dog in front of the farmhouse until it came charging at him, big and dark and loud. Percy crossed over to the other side of the road, but the dog came on, jaws wide and teeth flashing. Starting to run, Percy stumbled on the broken shoulder, breathing hard, feeling scared, like he was scared of the car in Guenther's driveway, always scared, scared again, scared now of a dog. A grown-up person, scared of a dog. Percy stopped, picked up pieces of broken pavement and threw. The rocks were too small; most of them missed and scattered across the road, but the dog stopped. Percy scrabbled for more rocks, bigger ones, and walked toward the dog, throwing and not missing, throwing hard, his teeth gritted, and now the dog was yelping and retreating, but Percy didn't stop, he found more rocks, he kept throwing, he kept throwing even after the dog turned and ran, he kept throwing until a car passed and he saw the faces in the window staring at him, staring at him like he was crazy.

Percy waited until eight o'clock that night before starting out. It made sense to begin in town, and then, if he had to, try the bars farther out. The streets looked familiar, but some things had changed. Where there should have been a doorway was a brick wall, and where there still *was* a doorway a closed sign dangled. That was okay. Percy didn't expect things to be the same; it was so long ago, he'd been just a little kid, sent to look for Guenther when he drank too late. Percy was older now. He'd changed, the town had changed. Maybe Guenther had changed too, but Percy didn't think so.

Two blocks later, he found the Worthington Tap Room where it always was. The dark, narrow interior was the same, except for a new flat screen TV on the wall. The row of heads at the bar turned to see who came in—that was the same too, the part he always hated, the faces looking at him. Percy glanced around quickly and left.

There weren't many places left to drink in downtown Worthington, and Percy walked all the way out to the bowling alley before giving up. No one tonight looked anything like Guenther, or how he used to look. Percy thought about that as he headed back toward the Y.

The last stop was Charlie's, or what used to be Charlie's, the one with the pool table in the back. When he stepped inside, the bartender caught his eye, but Percy's gaze slid past him. One of the men near the pool table spun slowly, and in that moment, before he turned around enough for Percy to see him clearly, he could have been Guenther. It was only a few seconds, but Percy kept staring until he was sure it wasn't.

Percy thought he wouldn't be able to sleep, but he did, right away. It was later when he woke up and couldn't quiet his mind. He rose and sat in the chair, looking out the small window at the streetlight. If it *had* been Guenther, what would Percy have done? He wasn't sure what he wanted to say, or do, but he knew it couldn't happen in front of other people.

MALDEN

Historic Wellind, the sign announced, but the town had a new face, the tall brick buildings restored, the main street lined with new lampposts, hanging baskets of blooming plants. Malden drove past art galleries, a coffeehouse, and the Wellind Hotel, founded 1865 according to the sign out front, now a brewpub with outside tables.

The other side of town was like the flip side of a coin; nothing had been renovated in years. The house he was looking for was all too similar to the others he'd visited—small and square and poorly kept up. Half-hidden by large trees, a pickup parked on the lawn. A man in a black t-shirt, his gray hair skinned back in a ponytail, squinted at Malden from the top step of the porch.

Malden halted at the bottom. "Is Sam Grimble home?"

"You serving papers?"

"No, no papers. It's a personal matter."

The man folded his arms across his chest. "Well, he's still not here. He won't be back for a while, maybe, I don't know, tomorrow." His eyes shifted from Malden to his car and back. "Maybe I can help."

Malden hesitated.

"I'm his brother," the man added, as if that made a difference.

Malden studied the tattoo that snaked up the man's arm. He had little hope for this stop. The name was presumably from an early time in Percy's life, his recollections vague, but Malden could be wrong. There was no clear chronological order to Percy's memories. As with most cases, therapy with Percy had skipped all over the board—past, present, and future constantly on stage, sometimes speaking in each other's voices. "I'm looking for a man Sam Grimble used to know. Robert Percy."

The man thought for a moment. "Never heard that name."

"He fostered with the Grimble family when he was a boy. I thought he might have come to visit."

"Foster kid? There were never any foster kids around here. Too many of our own." The man laughed. "You must of got the wrong Grimbles, mister."

Malden considered this. "Are there others around here?"

"Not in this town. Just us."

He stood there watching even after Malden was back in his car, so Malden drove farther into the neighborhood of small bungalows before pulling over to review his papers. One final name, Deyer, if that's how it was spelled.

A door slammed, and Malden looked up. Across the street, a woman walked into a garden, started to work between rows of beans and tomatoes. His mother would never garden like that, in sandals and shorts, bright flowered blouse. She'd always worked in the same old clothes, like a uniform—dark pants and a long-sleeved shirt, faded from the sun. And this woman carried nothing with her, none of the tools or baskets his mother always took as if she already knew what she would need.

When Malden was young, not yet in school, he'd followed her around as she planted and picked and weeded. She gardened seriously, intently, as though there were something between her and the soil that was real, sometimes more real than her husband, maybe even her son.

As Malden grew older, he didn't have much time to help her, and he didn't want to. He would get home late from school, put his books on the table, and catch sight of her through the window. In the fall, as the days shortened and the nights chilled, she worked even harder, though there was less to do; most of the vegetables were already harvested, the plants turning yellow, then brown, dropping mottled leaves. Malden had hated how she worked till the end, acting like the last few green tomatoes or the tiny peppers still had time, as if they didn't know, as if she didn't know, they had run out of summer.

One late fall evening, the year he started high school, he was struggling over his books, lights already on in the house, when he heard her outside. Malden listened for a while before he finally went into the cold dusk, where she was unfolding old bed sheets.

"What are you doing?" He knew what she was doing—he felt the frost already gathering in the air above, ready to drop down on the green tomatoes and the lettuces and the remaining cucumbers—but he said it to let her know he was older now, old enough to see how senseless it was to care about these last few after so much had been picked and eaten or canned and frozen. But then he helped her anyway, draping the sheets, turning the garden into rows of long, reclining ghosts, his fingers growing numb. After a few minutes, she took off one of her gloves and tossed it to him, and he was about to toss it back when something in her face, or the way she threw it, changed his mind, and he slid it on, still warm from her hand. They continued working together like that, one hand gloved, the other cold.

By the time Malden was a senior, she'd winnowed the garden down to a few tomato plants along the side of the garage. Not long after that, she was diagnosed with the cancer, and that was the end of a lot of things.

The woman straightened up and suddenly saw Malden. He stared back blankly before realizing where he was. He headed back toward the center of town, but slowly, with a strange reluctance; he couldn't seem to drive any faster. Pulling up to a stop sign when he reached the main street, he sat there so long a car behind him honked. He crossed into another neighborhood, turning left, then right, then left, coasting by older homes now, large, with a solid midwestern look, following the street until he was driving alongside a long, open stretch of grass, tall trees arching overhead—a park.

Suddenly tired, as if he hadn't slept in days, Malden pulled over and stopped the car, dropped his head back against the seat. He must have closed his eyes a moment, drifted off, because then he jerked awake, alarmed. Getting out of the car to stretch, to think what should be next, he found himself walking across the grass, following a narrow path of coarse stone, the sun low and the light softer now. The ground rose up into a small hill; from the top Malden looked down on rows of headstones. It wasn't a park; it was cemetery—a newer section, judging from the neat rows of nearly uniform stones. He stood watching the sky change behind the trees, the light fading, before turning back.

Somewhere along the way, he started thinking about Amy, that morning at the airport, waiting with her. Amy in a bright jacket and scarf, her body grown stockier at college, the new weight making her look mature; her face flushed from their goodbyes, her cheek against his.

Malden stumbled, caught himself, but when he got back to the car he had to lean against the side, catch his breath against the sudden sharp longing for his daughter.

10

There was not only coffee and tea the next morning, there was an open box of donuts. "Help yourself." The woman behind the counter smiled. She was older than the man from yesterday, lots of white hair, even nicer. So far no one had said a word about religion. Maybe the bus driver had it wrong.

Percy took his coffee to the park across the street, sat on a bench while the morning light rose across the tall brick front of the Worthington Hospital. It looked different. Probably they'd remodeled it. Finishing his donut, he watched people going in and out the glass doors. The hospital bothered him, and he wondered about the inside, if that was different too.

He was standing outside the doors, trying to see in, when suddenly they slid open. Percy stepped back, stumbled against someone. "Watch it there." The old man's voice was harsh. Percy apologized and hurried inside, though he hadn't intended to. His clothes weren't very clean, his shoes still dusty from the gravel pit. Everything in a hospital should be clean.

Nothing was familiar—the wide information desk, the elevators in the corner, the clusters of chairs and potted plants. Percy was blocking the way, people walking around him, but he couldn't seem to move. A security guard came toward him, but before he reached Percy, someone else touched his arm.

"May I help you?" asked a short woman in a dark blue jacket. She considered him from behind her large round glasses. "Are you here to see someone?"

Percy nodded, but then shook his head. He couldn't talk.

"Let's go sit down, shall we?"

Percy followed her, her dark blue pants and her dark jacket, to the chairs in the corner.

"Now then." She sat facing him and folded her hands in her lap. She looked relaxed, as though she could wait like that all day.

Her round face and round glasses were comforting somehow. She had short curly dark hair and a shiny nametag on her jacket that read D. Bretherest, Ass't. Director.

He swallowed. "I used to come here, to visit someone. A long time ago, but I'm not sure now. It looks different, like it was all changed?"

D. Bretherest glanced around. "Not much. New paint, new furniture, but essentially it's the same old place." She studied him. "Was it someone in your family?"

"He was my brother. Well, not really. He was my foster brother, but we were like brothers. He hit his head, and then he had a seizure. I used to come here and visit him." Percy's eyes started to burn. "And then he died."

"I'm sorry," the woman said, her voice quiet. "I'm very sorry."

Gripping his hands together tightly, Percy blinked, blinked again.

A moment later, she asked in the same gentle voice, "You were very young then?"

"No. I was ten, nearly eleven. Robbie was young. He was only seven."

"Did he pass away here?"

"They took him somewhere else. But before then, I visited him. I used to come and see him here. But maybe it wasn't here."

D. Bretherest's brow wrinkled. "If you wanted to make sure where and when your foster brother died, death records are public. You could start at the library; they could help you access the records on computers there."

Percy stared at her.

"But maybe I can help you." She pulled a small notebook out of her pocket and unhooked the tiny silver pen attached to one side.

"His name was Robbie Duncan," he said before she could ask.

She wrote it down. "About twenty years ago? Let's say early 1990s. And may I ask your name?" She jotted a few more things before she closed the little book and rose.

"Medical records are confidential, Mr. Percy. I can't promise I'll have much to tell you, but I'll see. Why don't you wait in the cafeteria? I'll find you down there." She directed him toward a hallway and told him to follow the signs.

Percy chose a table in the back, settled himself with a bag of chips and a soda. There weren't many visitors this early. Other tables were occupied mostly by hospital workers in blue pants and shirts. He didn't watch the clock, but it wasn't long before D. Bretherest walked in. He waved to make sure she saw him.

Sitting down with a cup of tea, she added sugar but not milk like Miss Mueller. Tea with Miss Mueller seemed like a long time ago.

"I can confirm some of what you remember, Mr. Percy," she said after taking a sip from her cup. "Robbie Duncan passed away from complications resulting from a head trauma in 1994, not here in this hospital, but at one down in Detroit. You can find all this in the public records, you know."

Percy nodded, but he knew he would never look.

"But Robbie Duncan was only here for a very brief time, at most twenty-four hours, in intensive care. He was moved to Detroit as soon as possible. He had a chance, but not here." She paused and held Percy's gaze. "If you did visit someone here, it wasn't Robbie Duncan."

The cafeteria was air-conditioned, but Percy felt himself break out in a sweat.

D. Bretherest didn't seem to notice. She sipped more tea, and then she was talking again, telling him that it was very easy to mix up memories, reminding him that he had been very young.

Percy wasn't listening. "Is there another hospital around here?"

"Not in Worthington. There's Hyborn, the state hospital outside of town, but that's only for mentally ill or emotionally disturbed adults. Not for a child with a head injury and seizures." She paused. "Are you okay, Mr. Percy?"

He pushed back his chair and thanked her, heading for the exit sign. He didn't remember the walk back to the Y, or up the stairs to his room, or closing the door behind him. He lay on the narrow bed, eyes fixed on the ceiling. As soon as she'd said Hyborn, Percy knew all about it—knew where it was, knew the big trees in the front lawn, knew the wide driveway that curved first to the right and then to the left. Knew how the big stone buildings looked in the morning, how the hallways looked in the middle of the night, knew what a piece of the sky looked like if you were lying in one of the beds with your head turned toward the window. Percy knew these things, but not why they made him feel this way, not just scared, but alone, so alone he could hardly stand it.

Three hours later, Percy was downstairs again, asking the woman at the counter if there were any buses out to Hyborn.

She eyed him curiously. "There's a shuttle bus, leaves from Worthington Hospital when the shifts change, around four o'clock. Some of the people at the hospital also work at Hyborn. I suppose you could ask for a ride."

Percy was waiting when the shuttle pulled up. After the workers, just two, got in, he stepped forward and talked to the driver. Percy offered to pay, but the driver just waved him in.

The ride was short, so Percy had no time to prepare for the sight of the hospital, tall white pillars, wide stone buildings. He gripped his hands tightly as they pulled to the front entrance and tried not to look up at the rows of windows above his head.

The small entry area was the opposite of Worthington Hospital's wide, sunny lobby. Not much had changed—the front desk in one corner, two chairs in another. The woman behind the desk looked startled. Percy wondered why; he had showered and shaved and changed his shirt.

"There's no visiting hours today." She had a scratchy voice like she smoked too much, and her face was very tan.

"I'm not here to see anyone," Percy explained. "I need to find out about someone who was here a long time ago. He was my brother."

Her expression was professional now, smooth and blank. "How long ago?"

He told her, and she wrote the years on a piece of paper. "And his name?"

"Robbie Duncan."

She asked for Percy's name too, and he waited for her to ask why the last names were different, but she didn't. She rolled away in her chair and spoke into the phone, her voice so low Percy couldn't hear what she said.

"Someone will be down shortly. You can wait in the visitors' room." She indicated a doorway that opened into a small space with chairs, a sofa, and a little table with magazines. Percy sat on the sofa, which looked new. All the furniture in the little room looked new, like not many people ever sat here, visiting. Percy focused on the picture on the wall, a painting of green hills, until a man, dressed in a suit and tie like a businessman, walked in.

He took the chair opposite, opened a notebook, and looked at Percy. Percy looked back at the narrow face, the small dark eyes. The man didn't look friendly; he looked busy, like he had been doing something and wanted to get back to it.

He introduced himself as Mr. Follet, director of the Hyborn Institute, and started to ask questions: where Percy was from, why he was here, why Robbie Duncan had been here. He wrote things in his notebook and watched Percy closely, which made Percy nervous. Percy knew he was talking too much.

"And where is Robbie Duncan now?" the man interrupted.

The question hit Percy like a blow. "He isn't anywhere," he finally stammered. "He's dead. He died in 1994."

The man closed the notebook, tapped it on his knee. "You do understand that even if your brother was here—which is highly doubtful;

this was never a place for children—we can't just give out information about patients, even if they have passed away." He stood. "Do you have any identification, Mr. Percy?"

Tugging his wallet from his pants, he took out his driver's license and handed it to the man.

"I'll be back in a moment."

Percy sat back down with his wallet in his hand, his fingers worrying the worn leather. If he stayed much longer in Worthington, he wouldn't have enough money to get home. Percy thought about his apartment. He didn't usually call it home, so it was strange he would think of it that way now. Suddenly he felt like he was going to be sick, and he rose to look for a restroom, but then Mr. Follet was back, handing him his license, waiting while Percy fumbled with his wallet again. When Percy finished, he spoke.

"According to our records, no one named Robbie Duncan ever stayed here. However, we do have record of a child, a boy, being here for just a few months, in 1994. But it wasn't Robbie Duncan." He made a strange motion with his mouth then, almost a smile. "The boy was named Robert Percy."

Mr. Follet continued to speak, but Percy didn't hear the words; all he heard was the noise in his head, dark noises, things crashing and tumbling, things he didn't *want* to hear. Falling back into the sofa, he buried his face in his hands, as if he could hide, as if he could bury himself away, like Robbie, dead and in the ground.

Percy wasn't sure how long he stayed that way, his head in his hands. When he wiped his eyes and looked up, Mr. Follet was gone, and a man in a white coat with a clipboard of papers sat in the chair. He looked Chinese, but you never knew; there were so many different kinds of Asian people, and many of them were Americans anyway, so it was best not to ask. The small, tough girl at work had lectured him loudly about how her people had been in America for more than a hundred years and that was longer than most people who called themselves Americans, and then she'd asked how long had *his* family been in this country, anyway? Percy had no answer to that.

When the new man spoke without an accent, Percy decided he must be American. "I'm Dr. Chen. How are you feeling, Mr. Percy? Better?"

Percy straightened up on the sofa.

"No hurry, Mr. Percy. You might want to rest a few minutes more. You had quite a shock." His expression was concerned.

Percy took a deep breath. "You don't have to call me Mr. Percy."

"Fine." The doctor nodded. "Robert." He looked down at his papers for a moment. "I must apologize for the way in which you were given the information." He spoke slowly, as if he were thinking at the same time. "It should have been communicated more carefully."

Percy told him it was okay. He knew Mr. Follet hadn't meant to upset him.

The doctor raised one eyebrow slightly. "According to our records, you were here nearly three months. Unusual to have a child here. Very unusual." He frowned, but then his face relaxed, and his forehead was smooth again. "I assume it was an emergency situation; perhaps there was no other alternative at that particular time." He cocked his head. "Do you remember now, Robert?"

"Some," Percy answered. "I thought I was here to visit Robbie. But that wasn't true."

Steepling his hands in front of him, the doctor confirmed, "You were admitted for a very serious depression, thought to be life-threatening. You had been refusing to eat for some time. You apparently didn't talk. You just slept. The cause was thought to be grief, the death of another child." His gaze was probing. "Seizures can look very violent. It must have been very upsetting."

Silence then, a long one.

"Robert?"

Percy squeezed his eyes shut. Robbie on the floor, arms waving and legs kicking.

"There's not much more here. Treatment apparently consisted of weekly meetings with one of the doctors. There is no record of medications used. In any case, you improved significantly, and they discharged you back to Family Services."

Suddenly Percy smiled, but he couldn't explain what had appeared in his head: the bald man in his robe and slippers, the one with the wet eyes and the scaly patches on his skin, sitting outside on the bench, always on the same bench. They were watching a man on a large green tractor mow the lawn, and the man was saying, "You want to get out of here?" as if Percy had asked. "Start acting like a kid. You know, a normal kid. Throw rocks, kick stuff, climb trees, make noise. Act bored. Mouth off. Tell them you want candy. Tell them you want to watch cartoons instead of that crap that's always on TV. You know." The funny part was that Percy didn't know. He had never been one of those kids.

"Why did you come back to this hospital, Robert?"

Percy looked up at the doctor. "I don't know."

Dr. Chen folded his hands on top of his papers. "Mr. Follet is concerned that your inability to recall your time here might imply unpleasant incidents during your stay."

Percy thought about what he remembered. Dr. Evensen, his kindly face, his slow, deliberate way of talking. When he wasn't talking, his face looked sad. Percy's room was far from the other patients', but he remembered the noises at night, the smells in the halls when there were accidents. How one man was always doing things to scare him, and then laughing. How Percy always ate by himself, in his room. How sometimes the nice nurse brought him books and toys, but mostly he just watched TV.

The small wrinkles were back in the doctor's forehead.

"I don't remember anything bad here," Percy said. "That happened to me," he added, because he wanted to be honest.

The doctor gave him a direct look. "I hope that's true, Robert Percy."

There was a silence then.

"Is there someone at home you talk with about these things? A counselor, a therapist?"

Percy hesitated, but then pulled out his wallet. He found Dr. Malden's business card and handed it to the doctor.

Dr. Chen made a note on his papers and returned it. He slipped his pen into the pocket of his coat, gripped the clipboard, and rose. "I hope you will talk with Dr. Malden soon." He held Percy's gaze for a long moment. "I don't know the truth about what happened to you, but I *do* know the truth is never easy. Sometimes we have to bury it, or if we can't do that, dress it up like something else." He stuck out his hand, and Percy stood up quickly to shake it. "The woman at the desk can help you with transportation."

The shuttle bus had already left, but Percy got a ride back to Worthington in a service van. Two men in gray overalls sat in the front. They talked in Spanish, as if he weren't there, but that was fine with Percy. He looked out the window and thought about what had happened at Hyborn, but not to him. It had happened to Mr. Halsey, and it was bad—the roof, the sirens. Percy could have told Dr. Chen about it; he wasn't sure why he didn't.

Percy slept very late the next morning, but he was still tired. It had been a long night. He'd woken up a few times, thinking about Hyborn. Once he woke up crying, but he couldn't remember the reason.

All the coffee and donuts were gone by the time he came downstairs, but he didn't feel like eating anyway. He stood aside to let a row of small children file past. They were so short he couldn't see their faces, just the tops of their heads, some of the boys' shaved short, like Mrs. Guenther used to do to Robbie and him. Most of the little girls had ponytails, and one black girl had rows and rows of tiny braids. When one of the girls, a tiny freckled face, looked up at him, he smiled, thought about saying something, but the woman bringing up the end of the line gave him a suspicious look, and Percy moved away quickly.

He went back upstairs, sat on the chair at the window, and decided that a shower might help him feel better. It did, a little. He dressed in the last of his clean clothes. Percy didn't think much about that until he was downstairs again, paying the young man for another night. "The last night," the man reminded him, and without planning to, Percy asked directions to the nearest laundromat.

It wasn't a long walk, but it was into a different part of town, unfamiliar, a street lined with strip malls. The laundromat sat between a plumbing supply store and a pizza place. There was no one doing laundry, just a woman behind a desk in one corner, staring at a computer screen. The change machine was out of order, and Percy went up to the desk.

She was small and thin, older than Percy, but her hair had orange stripes, and her t-shirt had a skull and crossbones on the front. "No problem," she told him, handing him his change.

Percy sat in a row of small orange chairs and looked through a stack of magazines. Most of them were for women. Percy found one about cars, but he wasn't thinking about cars, he was thinking how strange it was to be washing his clothes in Worthington. Everything seemed very strange now, after Hyborn.

After a while, Percy asked the woman if she had a phone book. She fished it out from under her desk and watched as Percy flipped through, looked at the pages, checked the names, checked again. He handed it back to her.

"No luck, huh?"

He shook his head.

"Maybe they're not listed," she said. "Or they only have cell phones."

Percy couldn't imagine either of the Guenthers with a cell phone, but he didn't say anything.

"You should try the internet. White pages, you know?"

Percy didn't know, and it must have shown.

"I can check for you," she offered. "What's the name?"

He didn't want to say, but she was being nice. "Guenther." The name sounded strange out loud. He spelled it for her.

She typed, waited, typed again, waited. Then she shook her head.

Percy was folding his clothes back into his bag when she stepped outside, lit a cigarette. She stood near the door, and on his way out, he stopped to thank her.

"No problem," she said again. She blew smoke in the other direction. "You could try the county offices. Public records, tax rolls, that stuff."

While Percy was listening he was also looking at her hand, the cigarette, the line of bright lipstick around the end of it. Mrs. Guenther didn't smoke, but her sister Florence had, smoked a lot, and all the stubbed-out cigarettes in the ashtray had red rings around them.

Percy tried the bars again that night. One of the bartenders noticed him and said, "It might be easier if you tell us a name." A man sitting in front of a glass laughed. Percy left.

This time, he stopped at the bowling alley, even though Guenther usually didn't drink there—the bar too small, only beer. The lights were dim, and the place looked empty, but Percy heard the clatter of pins and saw two men playing.

The bar was gone, just vending machines now. Percy bought a can of soda and a candy bar. Some of the guys at work had a team, and every now and then he went along to watch. They never asked him to play, but if they had, Percy would've told them he didn't know how, which was partly true. He'd never learned the right way, and he was never any good at it, but he liked to watch the guys who were—liked the way the ball seemed to slide right off their fingers, spinning and rolling in the air even before it hit the wood. And the way they joked around, called each other bad names, but nobody got mad. One time, when they were really funny, Percy laughed too loud and some of the guys turned around and looked. When they saw who it was, they turned back. After that, Percy didn't laugh out loud anymore. When they were funny, he would grin a lot, the big cup of soda in front of his face.

These men were very different, serious. They weren't joking, weren't even talking. Percy finished the soda and candy on his way out. He didn't want to be late getting back to the Y.

A day later, I was still thinking about all of them. It was hard not to in Malden's office, with the photo of Joan and Amy somehow always in my field of vision, Malden's careful script on Percy's file in front of me. Maybe that's why I didn't hear him enter—but suddenly there he was, Dr. A. D. MacAllister, the wide bulk of him, contained as always in a full and formal suit, just as he had been in front of graduate classes. He looked even more like a prosperous banker now, but maybe as the director of a large and very successful group practice, his style was not far off.

And why wouldn't he have keys to the office? He paid for it, had to lease it years ago when Malden joined, all the upstairs spaces being occupied. According to Malden, MacAllister had been trying to move him up into the fold ever since.

I had closed some of the blinds against the glare of the late afternoon sun, but the light wasn't so dim that I couldn't see the shine in his eyes—very large, very round eyes—and the smile already on his face, not at the pleasure of seeing me, but at his success at catching me unawares.

"Sonja." MacAllister advanced across the room, and I barely had time to stand up and move around the desk. If he wanted to pry, he would have to be obvious about it. I crossed my arms and leaned back against the front of the desk. Even then, I was taller than he, something I always enjoyed; I knew it bothered him.

"I understand you're helping out?" He looked at me the way he always did, appraising, as if he were adding me up, adding up things about me I didn't want him to consider.

"A few patients. Malden said he cleared it with you." I must have sounded defensive, because when he smiled this time, he was truly enjoying himself.

"My dear Sonja." He rolled his eyes. "Have I ever questioned your qualifications? Haven't I asked you to join us here, more than once? David is very fortunate to have your assistance."

I hated the way he called Malden *David*, reducing him, and wondered again how Malden continued to work for this man. The beginning was understandable, given Amy's diagnosis, Joan's decision to be home for her. Malden had needed something not only more financially secure but much saner, less exhausting, than hospital work. After Amy graduated, I thought he might leave, but perhaps college was more expensive than I thought.

I shifted. "Malden should be back soon."

"I wondered if we might talk about that." He glanced over at the armchairs and then back at me, but when I didn't move, he sauntered to the window instead.

"He's been difficult lately, our David." He fiddled with the blinds and let more light into the room. "Missing meetings, hardly participating when he does choose to attend, distracted, irritable. Of course, David was never much of a team player." He flicked his fingers in a dismissive gesture. "But usually a valuable asset to the practice. Not lately, I'm afraid." MacAllister turned toward me, hands in his pockets now. "The receptionist, such a nice young woman, has come to me in tears more than once."

He paused, and I wondered whether he was thinking of his dear David or the nice young woman he'd had to console.

"And now," MacAllister said, approaching me, "this abrupt departure, with no definite date of return. So inconvenient. It would have helped to know more about the nature of this family emergency." He stopped a foot away and waited.

I was ready with my answer. "Malden doesn't discuss his family with me." That at least was true.

"Interesting. I thought you were closer than that." He smiled, unkindly. "Or maybe you used to be."

He let the silence stretch out. I was clearly supposed to fill it. I did not.

"We received a call yesterday," MacAllister continued, "from a psychiatrist in Michigan, wanting to consult about a patient of David's, a patient named Robert Percy. The call was referred to me, and I had to inform the doctor that not only was David Malden away for an unspecified period of time but that we had no record of a Robert Percy ever in treatment here."

I blinked.

"Of course—" He waved his hand. "—we all see people privately, unofficially, as it were. I do that myself, just for a few visits. I'm sure you do it too, for a friend of a friend, or a relative." He walked over to the bookcase, picked up the photo of Joan and Amy, looked over at me. "Or perhaps the daughter of a friend."

I wasn't prepared for that. How could he have known?

MacAllister set the photo back down. "I've called David and left a message at his home and on his cell phone, but I've yet to hear from him. I assume the Michigan call was in error, but I would like very much to talk with David about it."

"I might be able to get a message to him." I tried to say it casually.

MacAllister shook his head, smiled at me. "I think David needs to call me, don't you?" He headed for the door, but then paused, like I knew he would, and I braced.

"To be honest, I'm not sure how much longer we can—what's the word—maintain David, given these issues. Of course, this is all between you and me. We wouldn't want to burden him at such a sensitive time, would we?"

I waited a few minutes after the door closed behind him. I didn't think MacAllister would come back—it would spoil his exit—but I wanted to be sure of that before I picked up Malden's phone, scrolled through the directory of calls received, and noted the most recent calls from unfamiliar area codes. MacAllister always was an idiot about electronics.

When I finally had time to call the Michigan number, it was late; a machine informed me that the office of Dr. Chen at the Hyborn State Hospital was closed. It was even later when I was home in front of my computer screen, reading about the Hyborn. In the photographs online, it was not as foreboding as some of the older state hospitals, the asylums of the 1880s. Hyborn had been built after the turn of the century, but still in the formal style—the circular drive, tall pillars at the entrance. A more modern addition on one side hid an older wing behind.

I wondered how Hyborn had managed to survive. Most of the old state hospitals had closed down decades ago, part of the move to decentralize mental health services, driven as much by the discovery of new psychiatric medications as concern for the abuses and inequities of institutional care. The hospitals were replaced by community-based programs closer to home, an admirable idea had the funding at local and state levels continued. Cutbacks in services, changes in political climate, and a growing public resentment over tax dollars going to the needy—sane or otherwise—had resulted a different system, if it could be called that. A system in great need of change, given the increasing percentage of mentally ill individuals who ended up in jails, homeless shelters, and emergency rooms.

Malden's cell phone went right to voice mail, which could mean anything—avoiding another call from MacAllister, perhaps. I asked him to call me as soon as possible, said that it was important, but that was all. It wouldn't have taken a moment longer to mention Hyborn, give him Dr. Chen's number, but I was more than tired, still disturbed by the encounter with MacAllister, angry with Malden for putting me in that position. There were things I needed to say to him.

As I closed down my computer for the night, it occurred to me that I was doing to Malden exactly what MacAllister was doing. I was holding information hostage.

MALDEN

The sound of hard rain woke him, and that sound in a dark room had Malden up and out of bed, ready to pad around the house closing windows before the water could come in on the floors. Then he woke enough to sense the walls of the hotel room close around him, walls and doors, and outside his room, rows of walls and doors, and windows not made to open.

He got up anyway, walked over to push the heavy curtains aside, look down on the streets of Wellind. It was still dark, not quite dawn. The lights in the parking lot glaring, the black pavement gleaming wet. He thought about home, their house, wondered if Joan would come over and check the mail. Malden wanted her to do that, to come into the house, the house that she had picked out, searching right up through her last months of pregnancy until she found something they could afford. It was Joan who thought about schools and traffic and having a backyard big enough for a swing set and maybe a garden, and enough room for even more children, although those never came. The neighborhood of tall wooden houses dating back to the '20s had aged well, patched up but never reinvented enough to be trendy. It had been a good choice, still was, still could be. He wanted her to use her key, wanted her to walk through the kitchen, the living room, wanted her to see the things she was missing—if not him, then at least her things, their things, years of things they bought, made, used, enjoyed, laughed over, regretted. He wasn't sure why he needed to think she would miss them. It made her seem softer, made him feel more hopeful.

Watching the rain, harder now, bouncing off the asphalt, the rows of cars, Malden thought about Joan never coming back to the house, never living there again, never sleeping in the bedroom, cooking in the kitchen. Joan walking around some other house, under some other roof. Truly gone, nothing where there had been something.

The rain slackened, but in the distance he heard thunder, a soft, low roll of it, like a line of surf. Possibly the end of the storm, or just the opposite. Summer storms were unpredictable. He remembered his mother standing on the back porch, one eye on the sky, the other on the clothesline, sheets already flapping in the wind.

Then another memory, years later, but still long ago, a humid summer night, he and Joan young, not yet married, rolling around on the small bed in her student apartment, wind coming in the windows, a crack of lightening in the distance. Hearing the thunder, closer, the wind whipping harder against their bare skin, they kept on; he knew she felt it too, the storm advancing—something in the way she moved, fingers and legs—she felt it too but they kept on, the wind intense now, a howling pitch. Somewhere a door slams, but she won't stop, he won't stop. Sheets of rain slam against the windows, blowing across the bed, cold and hard against their bodies, but they won't stop, not yet, they can't, as if the storm has infected them with its insistence.

A few minutes later, they finished, but it was almost too late; the wind abruptly gone, the rain slowed to a sprinkle, and a sudden quiet, as if it had never happened, as if they'd made the whole thing up. They jumped up then, ran around mopping up the floor, closing windows, cleaning up the potted plants overturned, dirt across the carpet, newspapers flung across the room.

They never talked about it, even though later that night, when she was over at the desk, sorting through papers, and he was in the kitchen where a small radio sat above the sink, Malden heard the news, reports that a small tornado might have passed through the area. He stood listening, soapy cup in his hand, saying nothing, though he could have called over to her. He didn't tell her later, either. It could have been a funny story, something to remember, something they might laugh over years later. Instead it was something he kept to himself; he couldn't explain why.

By the time the sky lightened over Wellind, Malden had worked at his laptop long enough to confirm the address of a family named Deyer in Clanten, two hours away. It was still early, the sky pale, the roads empty when he left town, but he stopped just an hour later. It wasn't much of rest area, surrounded by farm fields, just a short stretch of grass, a picnic table, a small cinderblock restroom. Malden didn't need to use it; what he needed was to stop driving. He had known it first thing that morning, but he set out anyway, ignoring it like he ignored his face in the mirror, his eyes. Packing up, checking out, starting the car—though each mile now made less and less sense. His careful list of names, all people Percy didn't want or need to see again. Malden had nothing else, nothing in his notes, and nothing on the tapes. He never had.

Rolling down the window, he let the wind, already warm, blow in with the dusty smell of the fields. In the far distance, a truck rumbled. The sound of the wind was louder than the ring of his cell phone. By the time he heard it, it was too late. MacAllister's voice again, requesting a call back, clearly a request that shouldn't have to be made but for the generous, patient nature of the caller. There was another message before that, apparently left last night as Malden slept. Sonja had something important.

She didn't pick up when he called back. If he started for home this early, he could be back in Buffalo tonight. MacAllister could wait, but Malden called Sonja again, left a simple message: he was heading home, he would talk to her tomorrow, she had been right.

After that, Malden just drove, nothing more to think about but the road and the traffic. At some point that changed, and he was thinking about his father, a trip together after the man retired. Malden was still young, not long married, Amy a toddler, when his father pulled into their driveway towing a small camping trailer that looked even older than his station wagon. Malden stared at the faded aluminum and the tiny windows. As far as he knew, his father had spent most of his life in a suit. Malden never camped till he went away to college.

When his father invited him along for a weekend, Malden went looking for his tent and sleeping bag.

"It's just for two nights," he told Joan. "Maybe he wants to talk about my mother," he added, though he had no expectation of that ever happening. His father had always been a private man, and losing his wife so early had left him even quieter.

They drove south, down into the Allegheny National Forest, to a campground someone had told his father about, a quiet spot that early in the summer. They arrived in plenty of time to set up at a site on the edge of the wide expanse of water.

His father looked different now, as if being retired had changed him more than his wife's death so many years before. The old slacks looked too small, and the new weight hung around his middle like padding. It gave him a loose, careless look, at odds with the serious attention that always marked his habits. Malden wondered if there was some kind of health issue, but when he asked, his father said he was fine, fine, no problems. *Live forever,* he had said, and then glanced around at his immediate surroundings, as if to confirm his continued presence.

In the evening, his father had fixed dinner inside the trailer while Malden collected firewood. They sat together at the picnic table and ate, side by side, facing the water. When Malden asked his father what he wanted to do now with his time, the man hesitated.

"I'd like to help you and Joan more, with Amy." He sent Malden a direct look. "Amy's difficult, isn't she?"

Malden rubbed his temple.

"You were too."

"Really." That was the first Malden had heard of it.

"You wouldn't sleep more than a few hours at a time, even when most kids were sleeping through the night. You got colds a lot. Probably allergies, but we didn't know too much about them, back then." He picked up his bottle of water, studied the label, set it back down. "Not that I was there for much of it. I had to travel a lot those years."

"I know." Malden stared out at the water. "Mom never let you forget it." It came out with a bitter twist that he didn't mean, left him surprised and ashamed, at a loss for words.

His father spoke first. "Maybe she had a right." He stood, his hand on Malden's shoulder to steady himself as he stepped over the bench, but later, lying in his tent, Malden wondered how much was for balance. His father was a reserved man, and the way he expressed affection was always somewhat formal, constrained.

Malden hadn't thought much about that until he was thirteen and throwing a football with a friend whose father asked to join them. The man intercepted a pass to his son, who started a tackle that ended up a wrestle, both of them on the ground, and Malden hung back, astonished at the tumbling bodies. When the two finally fell away from each other, breathing hard, grinning, he slipped away as if he had no business watching.

He and his father never camped together again, but they saw more of the man after that; he was a great help with Amy those early years—babysitting, taking her out—until his health problems started.

They should have taken another trip, Malden thought. He remembered walking back to their campsite in the dark, quite a hike from the pay phone at the entrance, where he'd called Joan. Malden had turned his flashlight off, letting his eyes adjust so he was part of it, the dark trees, the shadowy road, once in a while the orange flicker of a campfire. He was past their campsite before he recognized it, spotted his father, a dark, hunched figure, sitting, staring into the fire. Something about him looked as if he had never been anything but alone.

The call from Helen Johnson came just as he pulled on to the interstate.

"Are you still in Michigan?" She wasted no words: she was in Worthington; Percy was there too, somewhere, and she had no time for questions. She could use his help.

11

Percy was up early, sitting on the edge of the bed, rubbing his eyes even before the music started for the aerobics class downstairs. Tonight would be the third night. He would have to move, and where would he go then? Tom Guenther wasn't here anymore; Robbie was dead, as dead as he had been twenty years ago. All that was left was Hyborn.

Percy reached for his clothes, the clean ones from the laundromat. He thought about the woman there, lipstick on her cigarettes like Florence Guenther's. Florence had lived next to the park, the Worthington Community Park, the one near the railroad tracks, tracks they weren't supposed to go near but that Robbie did anyway, balancing on the shiny rail while Percy looked back to see if Mrs. Guenther noticed. If she did, it would be Percy who got blamed because he was older; he was supposed to take care of Robbie even though Robbie never did what he said. Most of the time Mrs. Guenther didn't see anything, her head turned toward her sister where they sat at the picnic table. Florence lived in the small brown house on the corner.

Percy got up and dressed. The house wasn't brown anymore. It was white with green shutters, and the tree in the front yard was gone, but Percy recognized it anyway. He walked past it into the park, which was mostly the same except the trees were bigger, and the picnic tables were gone. No swings either, but the monkey bars were still there. Robbie could do them fast, swing from rung to rung, hand over hand without stopping. Percy couldn't make it past the first one before he dropped to the ground. He was too heavy.

Sitting on a bench, Percy watched the house; Florence probably didn't live there anymore. A car pulled into the driveway, and a woman, tall but bulky, and too young to be Florence, got out. She wore brown pants and a brown top that matched, like a uniform. Percy couldn't remember if Florence had daughters.

He waited a while before he walked up the front steps and rang the bell. The woman who answered looked older up close, maybe even forty. Percy talked quickly because she had a hard look on her blotchy face and her hand on the door like she was going to close it any minute.

"I'm looking for Florence. Her sister was Alice Guenther?"

She didn't shut the door. Instead, she looked him up and down.

"I used to live with the Guenthers. I'm Robert Percy. We came here sometimes to play in the park."

A silence drew out.

"Why Florence?" came the question, but not like she really cared to know.

Percy tried to sound relaxed. "I'm visiting, and I'm trying to find the Guenthers, and I remembered Mrs. Guenther's sister lived here. She was nice to us."

"She doesn't live here anymore," the woman said flatly. "She's in a senior apartment in Sparten. She moved there after Alice died. Six years ago." Then she added, "Sorry," as if she'd remembered that Percy might care. She stepped back and started to close the door.

"What about Tom Guenther?" He asked it too late, but at the last second the door paused.

"I don't know."

Percy turned away, heard the door close, and was out on the sidewalk before he heard her call out. She was standing on the porch. "My husband says he still lives here, out at the mobile home park."

* * *

The walk out to Shady Acres Home Park took longer than she said. He had to go back to the main street first, and then past the strip mall with the laundromat, then nearly out of town. The sun was high and hot on his back before he saw the wide strip of green grass and the sign in front of a cluster of oak trees. Percy followed the arrows to the office. The mobile homes weren't new, but many were decorated with flowerpots and colorful signs: Bill and Emma Thomsen, The Jacksons, the Holmes' Sweet Home. The man sitting on the porch of the one marked Office told him where Tom Guenther lived.

The paved road turned to gravel as Percy made his way toward the far end of the park. The mobile homes there were older, no flowers. There was no sign in front of number 53, just a man seated at a picnic table. Spread over the top of the table were parts and tools; he looked like he was repairing something.

The man's hair was white, and he wore glasses, and he looked thinner than Tom Guenther—but he was still a big man, and the arm that reached over to pick up the beer bottle was just as thick as Percy remembered. He walked closer; this man was clean-shaven, his hair neatly cut. Then Guenther looked up, and his eyes were still the same.

"I'm Robert Percy," Percy said, but he could tell by the way Guenther tilted his head that he didn't hear him. Percy said it again, louder.

Reaching up to touch something behind his ear, Guenther kept his eyes on Percy, so maybe he had heard.

"Robert Percy." Guenther said it like he needed to think about it, but he knew. Percy could tell. Something about his face had changed.

Percy could feel his heart beating. "I was one of the foster kids."

Guenther picked up the beer, peered over the bottle at Percy before he tilted his head back and drank. "There were a few," he said, setting the bottle down.

"Me and Robbie Duncan."

Guenther shook his head. "Sad," he said. He picked up one of the parts on the table. "Sad case, that boy. Put me through hell, I tell you. They investigated us for weeks, talked to all my neighbors, nearly cost me my job." He shook his head again, flipped the piece of metal in his hands, studied it.

"You killed him."

Guenther's face closed up, and then he was on his feet, moving out from behind the table, his chest filling out the t-shirt. Percy stepped back, but suddenly Guenther pulled up short, smiled. "You think so? Sounds like you're still making things up in your head, Robert Percy." He leaned back against the table and crossed his arms. "Maybe you need to go back to that hospital, talk more to the doctors out there." He reached for the beer.

"You made me lie." Percy's voice cracked.

"I never touched that boy, Robert Percy. Wasn't me. Whose fault was it? You forget that?"

Percy lunged, but Guenther had already stepped back and was swinging the bottle at Percy's head, and then Percy was stumbling back, tripping, down in the gravel, small stones pressing against his hands and knees as he tried to stop, but it was too late. He was too many years too late to change anything. Percy let himself fall.

NIELSEN

My Friday night shift at the hospital extended into Saturday, one of those brilliant sunny mornings where the light is too clear, too bright, prying into every corner; I preferred my days to start with softer edges. I was home, still up, too tired to sleep, when the email came from Charlotte Waring. It had not been a difficult search, she wrote. Any case involving the death of one foster child and the subsequent institutionalizing of another from the same home left big tracks in files and traces in memories, even after twenty years. The death of Robbie Duncan had been ruled accidental after a lengthy investigation of the Guenther family, but how Robert Percy, a boy of ten or eleven, ended up even temporarily in the Hyborn State Hospital in Worthington, Michigan, wasn't clear. Charlotte, ever the professional, did not speculate, but stated that given this background and Percy's current issues, she would most certainly agree with Malden's concerns about his patient as well as his own liability, considering some of the recent interpretations of the laws.

That was all. Not an extra word, not an added thought, nothing to dilute the intent.

I grabbed my phone to call Malden, but his message was waiting: he was finished, he said, coming home—I had been right.

But maybe I hadn't been right. Maybe I'd been wrong, very wrong, at least to have held back the contact from Chen. Malden's phone went to voice mail, again and again. I stood with the phone in one hand, Chen's number in the other, the email from Charlotte still on the screen, but what I was seeing was Malden, not as he'd been days ago in his office, packed and ready to go, but much earlier than that, five or six years ago, when we were still working at the hospital.

There had been an emergency. One of his patients managed to leave the ward, and though the man had been restrained and returned, the doctor on duty wanted to consult Malden. Malden wasn't returning calls, but I knew where he went on his lunch hours. He'd given up jogging years before, settled for the machines in a health club around the corner. He was easy to spot in the last row, as far as possible from anyone else, in worn shorts and a faded t-shirt. His was the only face not looking up at a television screen or down at a monitor. Apparently, Malden looked at nothing, saw nothing, not even me until I stepped directly in front of him.

It had been more than twenty years since I had seen Malden in fewer clothes than he wore to work. He'd never been tan, but now his arms and legs were starkly white, his chest and shoulders much thinner than I remembered, as if his body had started to retreat, to pull in closer, flatten against his frame. I felt suddenly embarrassed. I had no idea how Malden felt; his face, when he saw me, went quickly from surprise to apprehension before I could speak. When I did, his relief that it had nothing to do with Amy was painful to watch. I remember leaving quickly; I had seen too much.

I put down the phone, went back to the computer, reread the message that wasted no time, and took only a moment to send a thank-you before starting a search for flights to Detroit. Flying time was usually less than an hour. If I caught a plane that morning, I could rent a car and be in Worthington by afternoon. I wasn't sure why I was going. Robert Percy hadn't mentioned Worthington to Malden, not a word about any of it: Robbie Duncan, the Guenther family, Hyborn Hospital. How could there still be a duty to warn, to protect? And who did I think I was protecting? Malden, Percy, Amy? Certainly not Joan. Never Joan.

MALDEN

Helen Johnson's directions were accurate, but it took Malden four hours to get to Worthington and find the small café, empty this late in the afternoon except for the woman there to meet him. She looked smaller and older than she had a week ago, and when she reached for her coffee, her hand shook noticeably. But her voice was sure, her words unrepentant as she explained why she hadn't revealed Percy's history in Worthington. She took promises of confidentiality very seriously, as foster parents are expected to, and—she looked at him sharply, sparing nothing—if Robert had wanted Malden to know, he would have told him.

"Robert had reasons," Malden replied. "But they weren't about me. He told me everything else."

"This was different," Helen Johnson stated. "Someone died." She stopped when the waitress appeared, waited until Malden finished ordering. "I got a call from my cousin's daughter. A man came to the house, calling himself Robert Percy, asking about the Guenthers. I got here as soon as I could." She picked up her cup, sipped, grimaced, and set it back down.

"I never heard of the Guenthers," Malden had to admit.

Pushing her cup away, she wiped at the table in front of her with a napkin, as if she needed a few minutes. "You know about Robbie Duncan? The other foster boy?"

"No."

Helen Johnson took a deep breath. "Robbie was younger. He died of a seizure after hitting his head. Tom Guenther, the foster father, said the boys were playing tag or something, and Robbie ran headlong into a big post at the foot of the stairs. Robert told the same story. Alice Guenther wasn't home at the time. Nothing pointed to Guenther, but he had a reputation. He was a mean man, violent when he drank. Not that Alice was any prize; she was my first cousin, and we all knew how she and Tom fought. She said she loved having foster kids, but I wondered how much she did it just to antagonize him." She closed her eyes briefly, and when she opened them again, her voice was harsh. "I knew those boys didn't have it easy."

Malden watched her struggle. There was no part of Helen Johnson that excused herself. Or, it seemed, forgave.

She continued, "I don't know where Robert is, but I know where Tom Guenther lives."

Malden checked his watch. "Have you contacted him yet?"

There was a pause. "I thought it might be good to have you along."

Outside the café, the sky had clouded over, and the air felt thick. Helen Johnson said she would drive. She knew Worthington, and she didn't slow down until they reached the narrow, winding lanes of the Shady Acres Home Park. She stopped in front of one of the older mobile homes.

Malden noted the empty driveway. "No car."

Helen Johnson opened her door. "Ready?"

She pressed the bell, and they stood together, waiting. After the second ring, Malden knocked loudly with his fist. It started to rain, slowly at first, big, heavy drops, but then faster, harder.

He followed her back to the car. She sat with her hands on the wheel as if she were still driving. Reaching for his phone, Malden realized he'd left it behind in his car.

Rain hammered loudly on the roof. "Why," Helen Johnson asked, eyes trained on the mobile home, "did you think Robert would hurt someone?"

"I wasn't sure he would. But it was a possibility."

"You came a long way for a possibility."

"That's true," Malden said. "Why are you here?"

"Do you have any children, Mr. Malden?"

He nodded.

"The first time I met Robert Percy—a family reunion here—he was sitting all by himself at a picnic table, watching the other children. It was the first I knew of Alice taking in foster kids. I went over to talk to him. He told me he had a little brother who was supposed to come too, but Tom Guenther said he couldn't. He had to stay home because he had been bad. I never saw a boy look so worried. I had a grown daughter by then, grown and gone, but there was little Robert Percy, just sitting and fretting. I started then, trying to make a case for Robert to come live with us. Of course we were too old. I was almost fifty, John already in his sixties, but I made a big deal out of being cousin to Alice, as if we knew the boy much better than we did.

"It took me two years to get care of him. If I had been quicker, none of this would have happened. But I was slow because I was tired, because it had been so hard with my own daughter. I hadn't done such a good job with her, and it took a lot out of me, and my husband too. When you're tired, you get selfish; you're not sure what you want to take on. It might be too much for you."

There was a knock on the window, and they both jumped. Helen Johnson rolled her window down, and a man, his face half hidden under an umbrella, peered at her.

"You waiting for Tom Guenther? He's on swing shift this week, won't be back till late." He leaned down farther to see into the car. "Are you here about that crazy guy?"

"What crazy guy?" Helen Johnson asked.

"The one who was here earlier. He went after Tom without nothing in his hands. You got to be crazy to do that. Or just stupid." He laughed.

Helen Johnson started to say something, but Malden leaned over. "What happened to him, that man?"

It was either Malden's face or his voice; the man stepped back, alarmed. "Who are you people? You know that guy?"

"I'm his mother," Helen Johnson snapped.

"Oh, sorry, I didn't know. He wasn't hurt bad. The police took him." The man was retreating as he spoke, already gone when she reached for the ignition.

"Drop me at my car," Malden said. "Is there a hospital in town?"

She told him where. "I'll go to the police station. I know a woman still works there."

Malden checked his phone as he started his car. There was a message for him, left three hours earlier, from a Dr. Chen.

12

Percy had been to emergency rooms before, but never as a patient, and never one as small or as quiet as the one at the Worthington Hospital. From his bed, he could hear the cops talking to the woman at the desk, saying Percy acted confused, dizzy, had trouble hearing. That was because of Guenther's loud voice, loud on purpose so Percy would hear him telling the officers Percy was crazy, Percy used to be in the state hospital, Percy tried to attack him. And the neighbor, a short, bald man, nodding and nodding. "I'm not pressing charges," Guenther said, "but you keep him away from me."

The doctor who finally came didn't look like a doctor at all; she was young, with hair short like a boy's, and when she craned her head to listen to his heart, Percy saw a row of small earrings pierced up the edge of her ear. Her fingers were soft when she touched his head, and her smile was nicer than that of the nurse who had taken his blood pressure and temperature. Before she looked in his eyes with the little penlight, the doctor warned him it would be bright. When she asked him where he lived, he told her about the YMCA and how he needed to move out of the room because he'd used up the three nights. He was worried about that.

She read some papers on the clipboard. "So you got into a fight, Mr. Percy?"

"No, no." He didn't want her to think that. "I don't fight. I never fight."

"That's all right." She patted his shoulder and kept her hand there while she told him there were no signs of concussion, but they wanted to keep an eye on him for a few hours. "Is that okay with you, Mr. Percy?"

Pulling the curtain around the bed, she dimmed the light on her way out. Percy dozed off, heard someone come in once and leave, but then he was lost in a dream, and Robbie was in the dream, Robbie on a stretcher, a long white stretcher, so small under a blanket, just a small silent shape, and Percy was yelling and yelling, and suddenly he was awake. The nurse was back, and then the doctor, and this time, behind them, was D. Bretherest, still with the same shiny little pin on her jacket, but this time the jacket was red.

D. Bretherest asked him why he was upset, and Percy felt bad he couldn't tell her. All he could do was lie there, tears on his face. She told him they wanted him to see another doctor, a different kind of doctor, just to make sure he was well enough to leave.

A few minutes later, the curtains around the bed opened again, and Dr. Chen walked in.

It was raining as they left the hospital, and it was pouring by the time Dr. Chen stopped in front of the YMCA to let Percy collect his bag. When Percy got back in, the doctor was talking on his phone.

The sky was darker now, thunder rumbling as the wind got stronger, pushing against the little car.

Percy watched the wiper blades and thought about Hyborn. He cleared his throat. "I'm not crazy," he said.

Dr. Chen kept his eyes on the road. "You are *not* crazy. You never were, Mr. Percy. But you've had quite a shock, as well as an injury, so you need to rest in a safe place for the night. You can't stay at the Worthington Hospital; I think Mrs. Bretherest explained that?"

"I told her I could stay in a motel. I have money."

"What did she say?"

"She said if I had nightmares and became upset, they might ask me to leave, or they might call the police."

"Do you think that's correct?"

Percy didn't answer.

Dr. Chen pulled to the side of the road, stopped the car, and swiveled to face him. "You're not coming to Hyborn as a patient, Mr. Percy. I'm sorry if I didn't make that clear. You're coming just for the night, as a guest—my guest. I live in one of the old residences. There's plenty of room. My family intended to move here with me, but there was a change in plans." He paused. "I hope this is acceptable to you?"

It wasn't, Percy thought, but he could feel the doctor watching him. "It's okay," he said finally.

Dr. Chen was quiet after that, driving carefully through the gusts of rain blowing across the road. They passed through the Hyborn gates, between the rows of tall old trees, branches bending and twisting in the storm. The doctor didn't stop at the main entrance. He followed a different driveway that curved around the side of the hospital to a large house Percy didn't recall seeing before, a square two-story building made of the same gray stones as the hospital wing that loomed above it. Dr. Chen shut off the car.

"I've been trying to contact your therapist, Dr. Malden, but there appears to be some confusion at his office. How long have you been seeing him?"

Percy had to think. "Since March."

Dr. Chen's expression was thoughtful.

Reaching into his pocket, Percy tugged out his wallet and thumbed through until he found the paper with Dr. Malden's cell phone number. He held it for a moment before handing it to Dr. Chen. "It's only for emergencies."

Following Dr. Chen to the doorway, Percy tried to keep his eyes down, but at the last moment, he couldn't help it. He couldn't stop himself from looking up, even in the rain, at the side of the hospital, at the long rows of dark windows that rose above him.

My flight was delayed, and the lines at the car rental were long; it was late afternoon by the time I finally drove clear of Detroit traffic and headed northwest. I should have turned my phone back on then, but I didn't remember until miles later, when I pulled into a rest area.

Malden had called when I was in flight. His voice was rushed, his message disjointed. He wasn't coming home after all. He had heard from Helen Johnson. She was in a town called Worthington, and Percy was there too, somewhere, and Malden was on his way.

I almost laughed. Serves you right, my mother would have said, though with her it was often not clear why this or that served me right. But there was no mistaking it now, was there? I got out to use the facilities. I could be back in Buffalo that night, only the credit card charges to remind me I had ever been gone.

I pulled back onto the highway with ten miles until the next exit, where I could get off and change direction, but I found out that ten minutes was too long, too much time to think. When the exit appeared, I sped past, and with drops of rain dotting the windshield and thunder rolling in the distance, I continued toward Worthington.

When I remember that drive, I recall nothing of the hours of rain or the streets of the town itself. I remember something different, much earlier in the trip, not far out of Detroit, when I reached the detour signs. I had to follow a long line of traffic off the interstate onto small, narrow roads. The storms that delayed my flight that morning must have been small and local, because the landscape here was dry—dead grass, brown fields, cornstalks already yellowing, their long leaves drooping like spent limbs. I passed no towns or villages, just houses scattered here and there, most of them oddly unsuited for their isolated setting: a low-lying '50s ranch house, a two-story brick colonial, a log cabin, mobile homes of varying ages.

At one point, when the line slowed to a crawl, I drove past a yard that looked more like a clearing, an open stretch of stubby brown grass in front of an old trailer. What caught my attention was the white plastic table—the round kind with a hole in the middle for an umbrella—

and the two plastic chairs, and the two women who sat in them, legs crossed, smoking, talking, as if they were seated in some sidewalk café in a busy city, as if they were sipping something other than Diet Coke from the two-liter bottle between them. As if they were somewhere instead of the middle of nowhere, and there were something to see instead of a brown lawn next to a strip of hot asphalt and a long, slow line of cars. I must have been staring, because one of them suddenly raised her glass to me. Or maybe not to me, maybe to the driver behind me or the one ahead, but I startled anyway and trained my eyes straight ahead until I finally moved past. I wondered later what they were talking about; husbands, perhaps, kids, their mothers, their jobs, if they had any. Certainly not about us, the long procession of assorted vehicles, our faces inside, gaping as if we were passing the scene of an accident.

PERCY

Dr. Chen was in a hurry, leading Percy through large, dimly lit rooms to a small upstairs bedroom, where he told him to rest awhile, that he would be back soon. After a time the rain stopped, the only sound the wind whistling through the window the doctor had opened a crack before he left.

The air that blew in was cool and smelled like wet grass. Percy got up to close the window, peered down at the long stretch of lawn, littered with twigs and leaves. The trees were bigger and taller, darker in the fading light, but that wasn't why he felt confused. The view he remembered was from a different place, a different angle and much higher up; his room had been on a third floor. And he remembered still another view even higher up, so high you looked down on the tops of the trees, and you saw far past the edge of the lawn, out to where the dark line of the woods started.

He touched the side of his head, still sore, and he saw Guenther's face as it had been just before the bottle hit—eyes slitted, teeth clenched in the narrow mouth. The man raised his arm, but then something changed and what Percy saw was not the bottle, it was the belt. He heard Guenther yelling at Robbie, telling him to hold still, Guenther yelling at Percy, telling him if he didn't help, it would be Percy who would get it bad, really bad, so bad he wouldn't be able to stand it.

Percy stumbled back and sat down hard on the bed. Something hit him in the chest, and the air went out of him, and there was nothing left inside except what happened that day. It filled him like it had when he was little, but it wasn't the same. He had grown but so had the memory, and what came with the memory. There was no room for anything else, and there was no way to run from it, nowhere else to go.

Downstairs, the only light came from a lamp on a small desk near the door, a desk with an old black phone and the piece of paper where Dr. Chen had written his cell number in case Percy needed anything.

Percy ran a finger over the careful numbers on the small white pad. Then he opened the door and walked out into the fading light.

13

MALDEN

The storm left the road out to Hyborn State Hospital littered with leaves and branches that were hard to see in the waning light. Malden drove fast anyway, though there had been no note of urgency in the doctor's voice. The conversation was brief; Malden guessed from background noises that the man was making rounds. Robert Percy was resting, he said. Not on a ward, but at the doctor's residence. If Chen was surprised to hear Malden was in Worthington, he didn't say.

The next call was from Helen Johnson. "Are you to Hyborn yet? I just spoke with the doctor who treated Robert. She said he was just bruised, nothing serious, but he was very upset, very agitated. They don't have facilities there for that kind of problem."

"Yes. Almost there," Malden said, impatient. "I'm sure he's in good hands now." He swerved to avoid a large branch.

There was silence.

"Mrs. Johnson, I understand your concern. I'll call you after I've talked with Robert."

She hung up.

Chen's directions were as precise as his voice; Malden had no problem finding the tall stone gateposts that marked the Hyborn entrance. The hospital was neither as old nor as big as he'd imagined, but it was still imposing—walls of massive gray stone, a row of tall white pillars across the front. He drove past a long wing that stretched out behind then turned toward a complex of smaller stone buildings. The expression of the Asian man who stood waiting in the parking lot, his white coat blowing around his knees, did not match his voice. Hands in his coat pockets, he looked worried as Malden approached.

"Dr. Malden?" He put out his hand. "I'm James Chen." Before Malden could respond, he added, "Robert Percy's not here."

Malden stopped, confused.

"I left him just a few hours ago. He seemed calm enough, but now he's gone. I've asked some of the maintenance staff to look around. It is possible he went for a walk."

Malden followed Chen through an arched doorway, down a wood-paneled hallway, and into a large, dimly lit room with a high ceiling, ornate moldings hidden in the shadows. The walls were dark and bare of decoration, one of the windows was shrouded with heavy drapes, and the carpets covering the floor looked just as old. The room was nearly empty of furniture; just two armchairs and a low table grouped under a pole lamp, and over in one corner, a small desk and chair. Neither man made a move to sit.

"I assume he is still on the grounds. He didn't take any of his things with him."

"May I see?" Malden asked. He followed Chen up a flight of stairs. When Chen turned on the light, Malden took in the duffle bag on the chair, the wallet on top of the dresser.

"I couldn't admit him," the doctor explained. "This is a state hospital, not a psych ward. But he was very distraught, and there was no one, no family or friends to release him to. So I brought him here. Perhaps that was a mistake." He looked squarely at Malden. "I've been trying to contact you. Your office didn't seem to know where you were."

"I know," Malden said. "I'm sorry." He walked over to the window, but the cloud cover and approaching dark left little to view. "Do you think he's gone back to Worthington?"

"It would be a long walk. But he might. Robert didn't want to come here. He was here as a child, you know."

"No," Malden replied. "I didn't know."

Downstairs, it was already dark. Chen turned on another lamp and motioned Malden to one of the armchairs before he settled in the other. The seats were oddly placed; Malden had to turn his head to see the doctor.

Chen sat very straight, his hands capping his knees. "It is my opinion that Robert is not on his way back to Worthington. You are concerned he will try to contact that man again?"

"Tom Guenther? Maybe. A week ago I was convinced that Robert was coming to Michigan for revenge, to hurt people who had hurt him. People he talked about with me, named." Malden put his head back against the chair and watched shadows in the ceiling. "He had reason for retribution, believe me. But he didn't try to contact any of them, the ones I knew about."

"Only Guenther, then."

"A person he never told me about. Maybe by the time he was ready to, I had quit listening."

Chen studied him. "You came a long way."

"I came because I thought Robert might do something that would damage my career, my reputation. I couldn't contact authorities; there wasn't enough evidence. But legally, I had—I thought I had—a duty to warn."

"Yes, I know the law," Chen stated.

Neither man said anything for a moment, then, placing both hands on the arms of the chair, Malden asked, "What happened to him here, back then?"

Chen folded his hands in his lap. "I have the file if you want to see it, but there is little detail. A diagnosis of severe depression, but no specifics as to exactly what type of treatment or therapy he underwent other than weekly meetings with one of the psychiatrists. No medications, apparently, which was prudent given what they had and how little they knew back then. Not that we know much more today; there are just more and different drugs available." He rubbed the side of his face. "I am very troubled now by this medicating of young people."

Malden started to speak, then stopped when the doctor continued.

"Robert Percy was here only three months, but that is a very long time for a child. He was housed away from the adult patients, but obviously there would have been contact. I have no doubt he saw and heard things he never should have." He paused. "Are you aware that Robert came here a few days ago?"

Malden shook his head.

"Initially I thought he had come back because of some ill treatment he received here, but he returned for another reason. You know about the boy Robbie Duncan?"

"I know about him now."

"Robert thought Robbie Duncan was the one who had been a patient here, at least at first. The longer we spoke, the more he seemed to remember his time at Hyborn."

Chen's cell phone interrupted. He excused himself and listened, his eyes on the floor. Then he thanked someone and set down the phone. "They haven't found anyone. I told them that my guest had gone for a walk and might have gotten lost."

Even in the dim light, the doctor's face seemed to shine, and Malden realized Chen was sweating. He had taken a risk by bringing Robert Percy unofficially to this facility. Malden was still thinking about the consequences when his own phone rang.

He listened to Sonja's voice, trying to understand what she was telling him. How could she be in Worthington?

Chen had risen out of his chair, his expression hopeful.

"Sorry," Malden said. "My colleague."

Listening to Sonja's explanation, he drummed his fingers on the arm of the chair until he could get in a word. "I'm out at the Hyborn State Hospital now. Percy was here a while ago, but he's disappeared. We're hoping he just went for a walk. I doubt there's anything you can do."

Still on his feet, Chen raised a finger.

"Hold on," Malden said into the phone.

"If Robert is walking back to Worthington, your colleague might be able to intercept him. I would be happy to provide directions."

Malden handed the phone to Chen.

When Chen returned it, Malden repeated, "I'm sorry."

"I'm not sure I understand."

"This complicates things."

Chen's smile was small and wry. "It's already complicated, Mr. Malden." He sat back down and checked his phone again. "I don't think we should discourage any help."

NIELSEN

When he opened the door, Dr. Chen's gaze skipped past me to the car. I shook my head. I'd seen no one on the dark drive from Worthington. The short man in his white coat, neat tie, looked up at me without surprise, his mind occupied with more than my height. I followed him into a large darkened room, where a few chairs clustered under the light of an old floor lamp. A room full of shadows, or shades—wasn't that what they called them, the ghosts left in rooms like this, hospitals like this?

Malden sat looking out a window, though it was just black glass now. For a moment he didn't seem to recognize me. Then he smiled, more like a grimace. "Come to the rescue, Sonja?"

Malden looked like he needed rescuing: skin chalky, eyes with dark smears underneath as though he hadn't slept for days. I didn't bother to answer.

The little doctor was moving behind me, sliding a third chair from behind a desk in the corner, pointing me to the armchair angled oddly away from Malden's. I dropped into the seat and sank another six inches into ancient upholstery. Chen perched on the edge of the desk chair. Malden stared at the carpet. I suddenly felt completely tired. I wanted to close my eyes, sink even deeper into the soft old cushions.

It was the doctor who finally spoke, explaining Percy's meeting with Guenther. "You know Robert Percy was here at Hyborn, briefly, as a child?" he inquired.

"I know," I said.

Malden raised an eyebrow.

"I finally got information from some contacts." I didn't offer more, and Malden didn't ask. I had nothing further to say, none of us did, and the silence seemed to gather around us like the shadows. A faint humming from another room stopped, and after a few minutes started again. There were the small sounds of Chen checking his phone from time to time, and the wind pressing against the windows, searching for hidden openings, secret gaps.

Malden spoke suddenly. "Are they searching the hospital rooms?" he asked Chen.

"Not yet." Chen cleared his throat. "I was hoping that would not be necessary." The ramifications hung in the air—the disruption, the impact, the subsequent inquiries.

Malden persisted. "When Robert was here, where was he housed?"

Chen's gaze sharpened. "Where?"

"Where in the hospital? Was that in the file?"

"I don't think so," the doctor replied, but he hurried to the desk.

"You mentioned it was somewhere separate from the other patients."

Chen flipped through papers. "There's nothing in here, but I assume it was in one of the older wings. They were seldom used, even back then." He set the file back down on the desk. "You are thinking Robert would go back there?"

"He might," I said. "But wouldn't it be locked up?"

"The outside doors, certainly, but there are entries from other areas. He might still remember . . ."

Malden stood. "We should take a look."

Chen hesitated. In his shoes, I would too.

"Dr. Chen, he's still my patient," Malden said. "All you did was keep him here until I could arrive."

The doctor's answer was somber. "I doubt very much that would help me, Mr. Malden." He opened a drawer in the desk. "We will need flashlights."

He found only one, but there was just enough light from the old iron lampposts for us to find our way along a narrow walkway that wound between buildings. We walked, an awkward threesome, through the pools of light and shadow. Closer to the side of the hospital the pavement suddenly gleamed, and our faces shone in the cold white radiance from much taller, newer light posts. Chen stopped in front of a large metal door, fished a ring of keys from his coat, and handed Malden the flashlight. While they hunched over the lock, I counted four stories looming above me, row after row of black windows. I wondered if Percy was up there in the dark with his ghosts.

We stepped into a long corridor, dimly lit by a line of emergency lights in the ceiling. I could see brighter lights at one end, but Chen led us quickly in the opposite direction. We hurried over worn linoleum that smelled of damp stone, past an endless stretch of closed doors. We were waiting for the doctor to unlock another set of double doors when we heard noises behind us, voices and loud footsteps. We all turned at once and faced the two men who approached.

"What's going on here?" demanded the one who wore a business suit, his face taut, flushed. The other man, in maintenance coveralls, carrying a large flashlight, kept his gaze on the floor. "Two of the staff were out looking for someone, a patient?" The administrator examined us: first Malden, then me. "Are they authorized to be here?"

"Yes," Chen said, his voice calm. "They are looking for their patient." His glance back held a warning. "This is Dr. Follet, our director."

"Who's missing?"

"None of our patients is missing, Dr. Follet. I'll explain in your office."

Follet glared at us. "I want to know who these people are."

"It's confidential," Chen replied. "I will explain in your office, in a moment."

Follet turned on his heel and stalked off.

As soon as the door closed behind the two men, Chen handed the flashlight to Malden and the heavy ring of keys to me. "You can't take much time." He turned and followed the men.

Malden headed off down the hallway so quickly I almost had to sprint to stay with him. I had no choice; the lights were much dimmer in this section, and ahead, the end of the corridor was cloaked in darkness.

PERCY

Percy wasn't thinking about light. In the basement corridors, there had been a series of dim yellow bulbs, half of them out, but enough so he could find his way through the wide tunnels lined with pipes and wires and hoses. He wasn't trying to remember the way, he was just walking, like he had walked through the black shadows under the trees and past the shine from the tall posts, walked around the back of the old building, past the loading docks, where the pavement was broken and the tall weeds came up through the cracks, until he found the small rusty door, still unlocked. And there had been some light in the stairwells, a single bulb at each landing. Up one, two, three flights—he was counting, and breathing heavily by the time he reached for the door and stepped out onto the floor where he had lived.

But when the stairwell door closed behind him, there was no light. Percy yelped, scrabbled behind his back, and pushed the door back open. The glow from the stairwell made little impression on the vast darkness ahead, and he straddled the threshold, listening to his ragged breathing. He heard the wind outside in the trees, and a humming from somewhere, like a vibration.

His room was at the far end, down there in the dark. He waited, and slowly his eyes adjusted to the gloom. On one side of the corridor, he could see where the rooms were, each one marked by a thin line of light at the bottom of the door, almost as if there were lights on inside those rooms. Percy swallowed. As if there were still people behind those doors, people in the beds behind those doors.

He knew that wasn't true, but it took a few minutes before he could let the door behind him shut. Quickly, before he was too afraid to move, he walked to the nearest door and wrenched it open. Thin grayish light streamed into the corridor from the tall posts outside. At the window, Percy looked out at the lights, the trees in the wind, everything black and white and gray. The room was empty—no bed, no chairs, nothing—corners shrouded in shadow.

Returning to the corridor, Percy moved steadily down the side with light showing under the doors, opening each as he came to it, one after another until the hallway was filled with the gray light. But his room was on the other side, and when he opened that door, there was only darkness, the window as black as the space it looked out on. He stepped inside anyway and held the door ajar until the glow from the hall showed him it wasn't anybody's room anymore. The bed was gone; so were the chair and little table where he sat and sometimes ate, sometimes drew in the coloring books one of the nurses brought—books for a much younger child, but he sat and colored in them anyway.

Percy had been the only patient on that floor, just him and the nurses who took turns sleeping in the room next door. None of them liked that; he knew they thought it wasn't necessary because he'd overheard some of them talking. But the old doctor said someone should be there at night, just in case. Percy was glad they were there. He remembered hearing them moving around, footsteps and the sounds of the bed. Those were good sounds, even when it was one of the nurses he didn't like.

He couldn't remember what else he'd felt those nights, maybe the same as now—the sick, cold weight in his chest but nothing in the rest of him. Nothing to see in the dark but Robbie and how he had looked. Nothing to think about except Robbie trying to get away, twisting and turning, his skinny legs kicking at Guenther, but not just at Guenther, *not just at Guenther*. Percy leaned against the wall and covered his eyes with his hands, trying to make it darker.

14

Each floor of the old wing was set up the same way: corridor, double doors, another corridor, then a flight of stairs. The only lights were in the stairwells. We walked quickly, side by side, the beam of Malden's flashlight skittering off the walls and the long lines of doors. As we entered each corridor, Malden would call out. "Robert? Robert Percy?" The first time he did this, his voice cracked, but after that, he sounded steadier. We would listen briefly, then move on.

When we reached the third floor, Malden, ahead of me on the stairs, stopped suddenly. I peered past him into the long hallway. Every door on one side was open, light from the posts outside illuminating the corridor. "Robert?" Malden's voice sounded different this time, softer, more careful. I walked in and out of each opened room— all the same; bare floor, bare walls, glint of white porcelain in a corner— while Malden opened the doors on the other side, used his flashlight.

"Did you open this one?"

I turned. He stood in front of an open door on his side, looking into a dark room.

"No."

He stepped inside, shining his light around the bare walls while I waited in the doorway. He stilled for a moment, as if he were listening, but all I could hear was the sound of my own breathing and, outside, the wind.

Behind the double doors at the end of this corridor, there were two choices: a short hall leading off to the right, or more stairs, these ones steeper, narrower, bare wood. Malden headed up without hesitating, shoes loud on the steps. I grabbed the railing and followed.

At the top, we stood together staring into the wide expanse of an attic, the ceiling disappearing far above us into a high peak. The air smelled dry and metallic. The small flashlight didn't penetrate far, but I could make out boxes, piles of pipe, a stack of lumber. When Malden called Percy's name, his voice sounded small, swallowed up in the space. We progressed more slowly now, more carefully, but I still tripped over a coil of wire and would have fallen if Malden hadn't grabbed my arm.

"Are you okay?"

The note of real concern turned me irritable. "I'm fine," I snapped. He started to move again.

"Malden, wait. How could he come up here without a flashlight?"

He didn't answer; he was shining the light ahead, on a large steel door, much newer than its surroundings, marked Authorized Personnel Only. I fished out Chen's ring of keys, and he trained the light on the lock while I worked, my hands shaking in spite of myself. When a key finally turned, Malden reached past me, pushing hard until the door moved. But I didn't. I stood facing him, my back against the cold steel. "Stop. Malden, I'll do this."

"What?" His head jerked back in surprise. "He's my patient," he said, his voice tight. "He's my responsibility."

I blocked his way. "I know, but I can do this." We were much the same size, my shoulders nearly as broad, maybe even stronger, our bodies closer together than they had been in twenty years.

"You think I can't?" Malden's eyes widened in disbelief, not that I would question his judgment—we had a long history of challenging one another—but that I would do it now, at this moment. I knew how he felt. What Malden was preparing for—what we both had been preparing for, well before that last flight of stairs—was on the other side of the door. Malden had no room for any other thought, but I did, plenty.

I held my back tight against the heavy door and made my voice steady. "If Percy's up there, and he's suicidal, and you can't stop him, could you bear it? Could you drive home, go back to Joan and Amy and your life? Could you?"

Malden flinched as if I had struck him, but it was enough. He dropped his arm. "And you think you could?" It wasn't a challenge; it was a question, professional.

"I know I can."

He was silent. I wasn't sure what he was thinking about, maybe his wife and daughter, maybe my abilities, my experience, though I doubt that. Malden knew nothing about my brother or the dark times that had followed. I wasn't half as confident as I sounded, but I knew it had to be me up there with Percy, and I would have said anything to make that happen.

He moved aside, let me go ahead, but I knew that whatever was left between Malden and me would never be the same.

I stepped outside into a strong wind still smelling of rain. Behind me, Malden stationed himself by the door. In front of me stretched a flat expanse of open rooftop, alternately black and white—the stark light from the posts broken up by vents and other shadowy structures scattered across the roof. I saw nothing that resembled Robert Percy.

Malden handed me the flashlight, and I eased forward, my feet loud on the gritty surface. I aimed for the far edge, skirting the vents, heat exchanges, an old water tank bound by iron hoops. I looked back once, but Malden was hidden in the shadows.

Finally I stood inches from a low stone wall that wouldn't stop anyone from falling, and looked down. The dark pavement below seemed both farther and much closer than I expected. I thought about how fast it would rush up to meet a body. My parents had insisted on an open casket; my brother's face was strangely untouched by what the fall had done to the rest of him. I thought I wouldn't look, but at some point in the service, I must have, because later I remembered features, pure and waxy, that bore no resemblance to the boy I'd known.

I stepped back from the ledge and the memory, and saw Robert Percy, a dark shape sitting off to the side. Not close to the edge, but not so far he couldn't be up and over in a few seconds.

"Robert?" I approached slowly, holding the flashlight low, letting my feet sound loudly, though I was sure he'd seen and heard me earlier.

Percy sat on a wide plank stretched across two roof vents, his shoulders hunched, his hands stuck in the pockets of his jacket. He stared at me for a long moment before swinging his head back to focus on the other side of the low wall. When I got close enough, I could see his face was wet, with tears or sweat, maybe both, his eyes huge, dark. I switched off the flashlight, and the gray-white light from the tall poles settled around us like a mist.

"Do you remember me, Robert? Sonja Nielsen."

He nodded.

"May I sit down?"

Percy moved over, and I settled on the plank. I left a good yard between us, but still I could feel his movements; he was shaking, his skin and bones shuddering in some stage of terror. I nearly lost my nerve then. There was no way, despite my height and strength, I could stop him. Percy would be gone, but he'd leave it with me, he would leave the falling with me, and it would be too much, despite what I told Malden, to bear.

I gripped my hands together in my lap and tried to speak, but Percy started first, as if I'd asked him a question.

"I came up the back way. Mr. Halsey showed me." His voice sounded hoarse. "He didn't mean to. I followed him one day. He was mad at first, but after that he let me sit up here too. Sometimes we talked, but mostly we just watched things." Percy hunched deeper into his jacket. "One day Mr. Halsey asked me to go downstairs and get his sweater. He said he was cold. It wasn't really cold, but he was shivering. He said he left it on his chair in the TV lounge, or maybe on his bed. It took me a long time; I had to be careful no one saw me.

But I couldn't find the sweater. It wasn't on the chair, and it wasn't on his bed, either. I looked in the closet too, and I finally saw it, all folded up on the bottom shelf. I ran for the stairs. I wasn't very fast, but I kept thinking about Mr. Halsey up there by himself. I was only halfway when I heard people yelling and doors slamming, and then I heard the siren."

Percy paused, wiped his face with his sleeve. "I thought he just came up here to be alone, not to do that."

I chose my words carefully. "Is that what you want to do?"

"Back then? I don't know. Maybe. I don't remember." Percy turned away.

"No, I mean now," I said. The *now* hung in the air, too loud, too soon. I should have waited.

But Percy continued. "I couldn't tell Dr. Malden about Robbie. Dr. Malden thinks I'm a good person. He said it was never my fault, what people did to me. He said I never deserved it." Percy dropped his head. "Maybe not before Robbie, but after that, I deserved it."

"They said it was an accident."

"That's what Guenther told them. He warned me if I said anything different, he'd blame everything on me, and I would go to prison."

Far off, I could see lights flickering, a car on the highway. I wondered how much time we had left, knew it wasn't much, that we couldn't stay there, up on the roof. But Percy had started talking, and I knew he wasn't going anywhere, at least not until he finished.

"Robbie wasn't supposed to be playing in the truck. It always made Guenther mad, but Robbie did anyway. I kept telling him to get down, before Guenther came out, but then it was too late; Guenther was there. Robbie jumped out and ran around the side of the house, and I thought maybe he'd be okay, he could hide out in the field till Mrs. Guenther came home. Then I heard the back door slam. I couldn't believe Robbie would go into the house. Guenther heard it too, and he smiled, and he pushed me into the house ahead of him and locked the door behind us. Robbie was upstairs. We could hear him." Percy stopped, rubbed his eyes. "Guenther told me I had to find Robbie or it would be me who got it, got the belt, got it bad, really really bad, so bad I wouldn't be able to stand it. His eyes were crazy. He wasn't drunk, but I'd never seen him so mad. I went up the stairs, but not fast enough. Guenther hit me on the back of the head so I would go faster. I checked all the hiding places, Guenther right behind me; he had his belt wrapped around his fist. Then we heard Robbie go back downstairs. He was running around the living room like it was some kind of a game; he was just making it worse. I chased him around the living room, and the dining room, and then I got his leg."

Percy's hands were fisted, so tight his knuckles protruded, white. "Robbie had skinny little legs, sticking out of his shorts. He was screaming and kicking because I was holding him down and he couldn't get away from the belt. But then he twisted really hard, and he did get away. He was scared then, running fast. He was running down the hallway, heading for the stairs again. I was right behind him when he turned his head to look back. I was so close I could see his eyes. That's when his head hit the post at the bottom of the stairs."

Percy put his hands over his eyes, and I listened to the wind and the noises he was making. I stared out at the treetops, the dark wet sky, until I felt the cell phone vibrate against my pocket. Just once. Malden's warning.

I wasn't ready, even with what little I could offer Robert Percy. What kind of choice did he have, the darkness in his head or the darkness on the other side of the ledge? Then I thought how old this choice was, how long Percy had been making it, year after year. "This isn't the first time." I gestured to the edge.

"What?"

But I knew he had heard me. "The other times, what happened then?"

He didn't answer.

"You made a choice, Robert," I insisted. "The same choice, every time."

"This is different," he choked out.

"Every time is different."

A silence fell between us. He looked out across that low wall that wouldn't have stopped him. "I can't forget it."

Of course you can't, I wanted to say. *Who gets to do that?* But I didn't. I wanted to tell him that sometimes the memories weren't this clear or this loud. I didn't say that either, because sometimes they're even worse.

"Maybe forgetting isn't necessary, Robert. Maybe you don't have to forget."

As silence settled again I remembered something someone told me, back then, though I didn't pass it on to Percy. It might not make sense to him, and also I wasn't sure, yet, if it were true—that there's a difference between staying alive and living, but you had to stay alive to figure out the difference.

I stood up and waited, waited for what seemed like a long time, until Robert Percy slowly unfolded himself and stood too. He seemed a little unsteady, and I took his arm as we walked. Before we got too far, and before I handed him over to Malden, I had to have one last say. I paused in the shadow of the old water tower and gripped his elbow.

"You were right about this time being different, Robert. You know something you didn't know before. You couldn't stop Tom Guenther—even now, grown up as you are. Who could, a man like that? So how can you keep believing you should have been able to twenty years ago?"

Again he didn't answer, which was fine with me; I had nothing more to say as we walked toward the doorway where Malden waited.

Percy didn't seem any more surprised to see him than he had been to see me. Maybe there had been too many years when people came in and out of Percy's life without warning or explanation, or permission.

"Hello, Robert." Malden stuck out his hand the way men do, reflexively, probably not even thinking how odd it looked up here in the wind and the dark. Percy took it just as automatically, and as they shook, I was suddenly ready to be gone, to be done with this.

"Shall we go back down now, Robert?" Malden asked, giving Percy a choice I wouldn't have.

I trained the flashlight on the door, but Percy pointed behind us. "I know a different way down. It's a secret, but I can show you."

Malden smiled, handed me the flashlight.

Neither of them looked back, and I heard Percy's voice start up as I headed alone down the stairs behind the flickering beam of the flashlight. While descending, I phoned Chen, assuring him everyone was safe and turning down his offer of lodging for what was left of the night. A wise choice, given the look on the face of the director standing with Chen at the bottom of the stairwell. Malden and Percy weren't far behind, I said. I didn't mention an alternate route, and when I got back to my car, I sent Malden a quick text as to where the two were waiting. Malden could fend for himself, but Percy didn't need any more troubles than he already had.

I drove all the way back to Detroit, watching the sky lighten as I neared the airport, but by then the weight of the night had settled on my neck and shoulders, and the thought of sitting and waiting for an opening on a flight to Buffalo was intolerable. I paid far too much for a room in the airport hotel, the quasi-elite surroundings lost on me, and sent the message I owed to Charlotte Waring. It wasn't the one I had been composing on the drive, and it wasn't the story I'd owed her years ago, the one that didn't have Percy or Malden in it, that I'd never even tried to tell. It was too late for that now. I typed a simple update: thanks to her help, the situation had been resolved before any harm was done. Percy was back under Malden's care.

I turned off my phone and waited for sleep to come. Despite the expensive insulation, I could hear the jets, and the sounds ended up in a dream about my brother's model airplanes.

15

Malden took Chen up on the offer of a bed, but after Percy was settled in his room, he followed the doctor back downstairs, stood in the kitchen while the man made tea. The room was updated but oddly arranged, the stove in one corner, the refrigerator in another, both far from the deep old sink and the bright new countertop. The tea Chen carried into the living room seemed an odd match too; the teapot and cups fine old porcelain, but the tea itself in bags, a supermarket brand.

They sat in the soft upholstered chairs and sipped while Malden relayed the story Percy had told him as he led the way through narrow stairwells, words echoing in the dim tunnels—Robbie's end against the stair post.

"Percy was trying to tell me months ago," Malden said, rubbing his forehead. "Long silences, missed appointments, calls at night. I should have seen, understood." Amy, six years ago, with her small fifteen-year-old face, standing in the bedroom, asking for a ride to the hospital.

"I have a daughter," Malden began as if the doctor had asked, and he explained Amy, her history, diagnosis, the medications, the current relapse. Chen's questions were few and careful, his observations thoughtful. It might have been the late hour, the fatigue Malden was starting to feel, or the way Chen listened, his face motionless in the small circle of light from the old lamp, his gaze often down on his cup while Malden's roved the corners and ceiling of the shadowy room, that started Malden talking about Joan.

At first, Malden spoke easily, as though he weren't talking about himself. Then he slowed, searching for words, and after that he was lost, stumbling awkwardly between past and present—Amy's empty room, Joan's merciless apartment, MacAllister's office, where there never seemed to be enough air. Neither Malden nor Chen had moved their chairs, so they sat at the same odd angles, Chen in Malden's peripheral vision, though from time to time the doctor shifted and watched him. But he never interrupted, even during the long pauses.

"I told Joan it was nothing. It just . . . happened. I can't make her believe that, but it's true." It wasn't true, Malden suddenly realized. It appeared clearly now, a series of choices starting with the first conversation. Moments when he could have walked away instead of following her to the coffee stand, instead of pouring some for her. When another man had joined them, someone who knew Malden, she excused herself, pretending she'd remembered something, but she'd looked at Malden first, and he'd known she wouldn't go far. He found her in a chair near the elevators, waiting for him.

Malden drained his cup, placed it on the table. This was what was left now, not the collision of flesh and bones, but the decisions in each place and at each moment when things could have gone differently. But he hadn't let them.

Chen poured more tea, and some time passed before he spoke, his voice quiet but very clear. "I am not in a position to comment, of course. You are not my patient."

Malden waved his hand.

"But I can speak to the way you appear to be thinking." He placed his cup on the small table, relaxed back in his chair. "You have been examining your action from its consequences, the impact on your wife, your marriage, possibly your daughter's health. These are the results, so you think perhaps you must have wanted these things to happen." He paused. "I am not so sure. We often set things in motion, sometimes major events, without intending to. If you had

165

meant to hurt your wife, endanger your marriage, risk your daughter's health, you would be a cruel, selfish man. If you never intended any of this, but acted without thought whatsoever, you would be a stupid fool. You are neither, Mr. Malden, and thinking in those terms is not helpful."

Malden stared down into his tea while Chen let the silence spool out.

"If I understand correctly, Dr. Malden, you intend to try to make amends?"

"God, yes," Malden said quickly. "Yes."

"But there is more, you know."

Malden waited.

"Assume," the small doctor continued, "assume your wife never found out. Would there still be consequences? Of course. But the consequences would be only about you, what you've done to yourself, what this will continue to do. You must also address that, Dr. Malden." He removed his glasses, polished them with a napkin, then replaced them. "It is never easy, this struggle; to understand, to reconcile our actions with who we think we are." He paused. "Or who we are trying to be."

The man sighed then, just a small sound that could have been about Malden, or maybe not, and rose to gather up the cups.

They said goodbye at the foot of the stairs, Malden thanking Chen for his help. Chen just smiled and thanked him in return. "For helping with Robert Percy," he explained.

Malden started up the stairs. "Thank Sonja Nielsen."

"You followed him," Chen said. "I think for more than just legal reasons."

Malden stopped and regarded the small man for a moment. "I was losing everything, everyone," he said simply. "I couldn't afford to lose Robert Percy too."

The next morning was cloudy, the pavement still puddled with rain from the storm, but the air was already warm. Malden stood outside the doctor's residence with Percy. In daylight, the hospital looked safe and orderly, the old wing just a building of faded stone and empty windows. Percy shifted from one foot to another, his duffel bag on the curb. Helen Johnson wasn't due for another ten minutes, but Percy had insisted on being ready.

Keeping his eyes on the driveway, he asked, "Does she know about Guenther?"

"I think so. She went to the hospital."

Percy frowned. "She doesn't approve of fighting."

"If you want her to know anything more, you'll have to tell her yourself," Malden said. "It might not be a bad idea."

By the time Malden had come downstairs that morning, Chen was already off on early rounds. Percy appeared as Malden was listening to Helen Johnson's message on his phone. She had already consulted with Chen, who agreed it would be entirely suitable for her to take Percy back to her home for a few days' rest. She was calling to inform them she would arrive shortly.

They had to scramble to get ready, Percy saying she would be early, and she was. Percy smoothed his hair down as the small car pulled into the parking area. Helen Johnson unfolded her frame from the seat and limped briskly toward them. Her face was clear, expectant; none of the fatigue and worry from the day before was evident. Malden rubbed his own face, unshaven, but she didn't spare him a glance. "Are you okay, Robert?"

"I'm okay, Mom Johnson."

She stepped forward and hugged him briefly. Then she pulled back, squinted. "Did you cut your hair?"

Percy patted his head. "Does it look okay?"

"Hmm." She finally turned to Malden. She seemed about to say something, but she just nodded.

Malden nodded back.

Percy picked up his duffle bag. "Goodbye, Dr. Malden. I'll see you next week?"

Malden thought about MacAllister. "I hope so."

He watched Helen Johnson reverse, turn out of the parking lot, and start down the long driveway. He was still standing there when the car stopped and both doors opened. Percy walked around to the driver's side, Helen Johnson to the passenger's side. When the vehicle started off again, Malden prepared to return to the house, but a flash of movement stopped him. Just before the car turned out of sight, Percy stuck his arm out the window and waved.

16

I had been back in Buffalo almost a month, the heat of August giving way in early September, the days still warm but shortening, the evenings suddenly cooler, before I got the email from Amy Malden. She was back from Europe, living at home, and she wanted to start therapy again.

"There've been some major changes," Amy wrote. "My father is living in an apartment. He and my mother are trying to work things out. I'm not sure what happened, but actually I'm not too surprised. They always had problems, no matter how hard they tried to hide them. I used to wonder if they were staying together for my sake. They obviously decided I was well enough to survive this. Which, in an odd way, feels very good."

This wasn't what she needed to talk about, Amy continued. She needed to deal with her relapse in Europe. There were issues to resolve, and she was looking forward to working with me again. Under the same conditions, of course—that her father and mother not know I was the one treating her.

My answer was brief, but I hope caring. I would be happy to recommend other therapists. I had decided, even before I received her message, that I didn't need the Malden family in my life, and they didn't need me, if they ever had. I still had family of my own, however damaged, and I was headed there next week, well in advance of my usual biannual visit. The boxes full of my brother's airplanes were already in the car. My father could figure out if they were still operable, and if it was worth a drive to the lake to fly them, again, over the water. Maybe my mother would come along; we could bring a chair for her. She could sit and watch, read her Bible.

I may have lied to Percy, implying how much of a conscious choice he had about staying alive. As if his muscles and his bones had no say in it, as if his feet hadn't made decisions of their own to stay flat on the gritty rooftop. As if his blood hadn't chosen to keep flowing, his heart beating. As if, however grim the half-life after a brother's death, it were not the body that determined to continue, despite the mind.

The previous week I'd heard from Charlotte Waring. She was preparing to present at a conference in Buffalo, said she was looking forward to seeing me there. She'd moved a few years ago to Ann Arbor, married, bought a house. She was involved in a research project she thought would interest me. So we would meet. It was as if at some point it had been decided we would be friends, or at the least colleagues. She, I realized, had been both. But she appeared to be offering the option; if I couldn't manage the former, perhaps I could the latter.

She was also interested in hearing more about Robert Percy, but I'm not sure I had much to tell her. Perhaps with Malden's help, Percy could figure out how to quit punishing himself, though this too is not so easily controlled, the habits of the heart not so quickly redirected. According to Malden's most recent email, Percy was making progress, albeit unevenly. "There are days when he can't say much," Malden wrote, "but there are days when I can't say much either, and then we just keep company, the two of us."

This was the second message from Malden since Michigan; the first was a brief and awkward thanks for my help. I hadn't responded to either. I was not worried Joan had told him about our meetings, or that Amy had revealed her history of treatment with me. Either way, I was the one who knew too much.

If the decision to keep living weren't completely under our conscious control, then perhaps neither was the tendency to frequently retreat from too much life, to turn away from the possibilities and the opportunities for a full, more vital existence. A tendency to twist away from the burn of love, the keen edges of joy, the comfort of friendship, cannot always be traced to events of twenty or thirty years ago. Maybe it was as much a part of us as the texture of our skin or the length of our bones.

Malden's email, the second one, still sat in my inbox, haunting my screen, as Malden most likely knew it would, until I finally responded. There were many things Malden didn't, and wouldn't, know about me, but he understood that I needed to know more about Percy, how he was changing, or growing. He understood my need to learn more about the heart—how a heart, if it wanted to badly enough, began to heal itself.

17

PERCY

Something woke Percy, but it wasn't the alarm; not at 2:00 a.m., the street outside still quiet, the window still dark. If it was a dream, it wasn't a bad one. His heart wasn't pounding, and he wasn't sweating. He was lying in his own bed, which still felt pretty good even after being home almost a month. During that first week, there were times he woke up and didn't know where he was, which town, which bed. And for a while things looked different, as if he had been away a month instead of just a week. Some things still did, like Joanne's face, as though she'd changed her hair or something.

Joanne had fed the cat and brought in his mail. He should have gotten her a nice present, but Percy didn't think of it until too late, so he just brought her a bag of donuts from the place on the corner. Joanne opened it and said, "Oh look, your favorites," and then she had to tell him that she was only teasing, which he kind of knew.

Joanne warned him she never saw the cat, although she kept putting out food. She said she hoped she wasn't feeding rats or something, and then she laughed. Percy laughed too but didn't think it was so funny.

When she asked what he'd done in Michigan, he just talked about visiting Mom Johnson, though the two days he stayed in Willits he wasn't sure you could call visiting. They were busy, going to the community college to get copies of his transcripts and talk to the advisors, using Mom Johnson's laptop to research welding programs in

Buffalo, and then the trip to the barbershop—just to even it out, she said, but now it looked even shorter. The last thing was the visit to Dad Johnson's grave. She had planted real flowers instead of plastic, so they took a little trowel, and he weeded while she picked off dead blossoms. She brought the watering can, the old tin one they'd had on the farm.

The welding class started last week, and Percy still wasn't sure about it. The teacher was younger than he expected and not very patient. Percy worried about being smart enough; he didn't want to waste Mom Johnson's money. When she called to ask how it was going, he must have sounded doubtful, because she said "You'll do fine" twice, and in a letter she wrote that she was sure the welders at the factory weren't exactly brainy. Percy thought she sure had that right.

When he asked at the factory to change his schedule to fit his classes, they moved him to cafeteria work, cleaning and carrying heavy supplies. Percy didn't mind; he liked being around food, and Angie, who was nice to him, still worked there. She was starting to look like she was pregnant, even though she didn't wear a ring and never mentioned a husband or a boyfriend. Angie saved him leftover desserts and showed him photos on her cell phone, mostly her family, some still in Puerto Rico. Percy didn't have a cell phone yet, but he was saving up for one. Mom Johnson wanted to sign him up on her plan, but he told her he wasn't ready yet. There were enough new things at once.

Percy talked to Dr. Malden every week—that hadn't changed—but he didn't cry as often or hit the pillows as much. Sometimes he still had bad days, and bad dreams, and he would always hate Guenther, but he didn't think about him much. Percy still talked about Robbie, but the more he talked, the farther away Robbie seemed, still there, but in the distance. The trip was starting to feel different too, like it all happened months and months ago.

But Percy still thought about Sonja Nielsen. He never told anyone what she'd said up on the roof, not even Dr. Malden. It seemed too private. Percy felt bad he never thanked her. He asked Dr. Malden if he ever saw her, and Dr. Malden said not recently, but he wrote down her address, said he was sure she would appreciate hearing from him. Percy hadn't written to her yet. He was still thinking about what he would say; he wanted to get it right.

He was falling back to sleep when he heard the noise again, a scraping sound, the sound of a small bowl being nudged around on a tile floor. He should buy one of those cat bowls with stuff on the bottom that makes it stay put. Percy thought about getting up and checking to make sure it really was Homeless and not some other cat that figured out how to get in through the bathroom window, then decided it was okay to be a little worried but not too much, decided it was good enough to lie there in his own bed and listen a while, to the sound of a car in the distance, and to the soft scrunching noises of his cat in the next room.

Acknowledgments

This novel would never have been written without the support and encouragement of family and friends, and especially Marty Naparsteck, novelist and teacher, whose constant advice and assistance made this book possible.